Enid Blyton

Bimbo
& Topsy

D0192460

Enid Blyton

Bimbo & Topsy

Happy Days

Bounty Books

First published in 1943.

This edition published in 2013 by Bounty Books,
a division of Octopus Publishing Group Ltd,
Endeavour House,
189 Shaftesbury Avenue,
London WC2H 8JY
www.octopusbooks.co.uk

An Hachette UK Company
www.hachette.co.uk
Enid Blyton ® Text copyright © 1943, 2013 Hodder & Stoughton Ltd.
Illustrations copyright © 2013 Octopus Publishing Group Ltd.
Layout copyright © 2013 Octopus Publishing Group Ltd.

Illustrated by Guy Parker-Rees.
Cover illustration by Alan Fredman.

All rights reserved. No part of this work may be reproduced or utilized in any
form or by any means, electronic or mechanical, including photocopying,
recording or by any information storage and retrieval system, without the
prior written permission of the publisher.

ISBN: 978-0-75372-579-5

A CIP catalogue record for this book is available from the British Library.

Printed and bound by CPI Group (UK) Ltd, Croydon, CR0 4YY

Contents

A letter from Bimbo

Hello, children!

I do think it's fun to have a book of my own, don't you? I've been looking through the pages, and I think I look very nice in the pictures. If you colour me with your crayons, don't forget to give me blue eyes, not green.

I do a lot of naughty things in this book – but Mistress says she wouldn't part with me, even if I were twice as bad. So she must love me very much, mustn't she? I hope you will love me too, when you read my book. I am sharing it with Topsy, the puppy. She will write you a letter at the end.

A hundred purrs from,

Bimbo

Chapter 1
The New Little Kitten

One day a little kitten arrived in a basket at a house called Green Hedges. He was a present for two little girls there, and how they squealed with joy to see him!

'He's not a bit like an ordinary cat!' said Gillian. 'He's creamy-white, and he's got a chocolate-brown nose, ears, feet and tail!'

'And do look at his eyes!' said Imogen. 'They are bright blue – like the sea on a summer's day.'

So they were. The kitten looked up at the two little girls with his brilliant eyes, and then jumped out of the basket.

'Mee-ow-ee-ow!' he said. 'Of course I'm not like an ordinary cat – I'm a Siamese cat, didn't you know? We are always brown and cream, and our eyes are always blue! I've come to live with you.'

He jumped up on to Gillian's lap. 'I haven't a name,' he mewed. 'You must give me one. How can I come when I'm called if I haven't a name?'

'We can't call you, silly, if you haven't a name!' said Gillian. 'Imogen – what shall we call him?'

'Paddy-paws,' said Imogen.

'No – that's too long,' said Gillian. 'What

about Whiskers?'

'All the cats in the garden would come if we called "Whiskers, Whiskers!"' said Imogen, 'because they've all got whiskers.'

'Well – let's call him *Bimbo* then!' said Gillian. 'Mummy once had a cat she loved called Bimbo – and this is a cat we shall love, so we'll call him Bimbo.'

'That's a nice name,' said Imogen. 'I shall like calling that. I shall often stand in the garden and call Bim-bim-bim-bimbo!'

'Do you like that name, Bimbo?' said Gillian, and she stroked the creamy coat of the new kitten. He nibbled at her fingers!

'Mee-ow! Yes – that's a nice name for a cat like me. I'm glad I've got a name. Now I feel real. You don't feel real if you haven't a name. Let me go into the corner over there and hide. Then you call me, and I'll come. I shall feel a proper cat then.'

He jumped off Gillian's knee and ran to the corner. He hid under a chair and waited. The two children called him loudly.

'Bim-bim-bimbo! Bim-bim-bimbo!'

'Mee-ow!' said Bimbo, and sprang out of the corner at once. 'I'm here! I'm Bimbo!'

And that is how Bimbo came to the nursery and got his name. He soon settled down there and grew to know everyone in the house.

There was Bobs, the big black-and-white fox-terrier, a kindly old dog who didn't seem to mind if Bimbo jumped out to frighten him. There was Cosy, a fat tabby, two years old, who smacked Bimbo when he was rude to her. There were the white pigeons in the garden, that Gillian said Bimbo was never to touch. And there were the grey doves in the big cage, who said 'Coo-coo-coo' all day long.

Bobs went out for walks with the children. Bimbo wanted to go too. But Gillian said no.

'You would be frightened of the cars,' she said, 'and the dogs would chase you.'

'Oh no, they wouldn't,' said Bimbo. 'Bobs doesn't chase me – and he's a dog, isn't he? As for cars, I don't even know what they are. But I'm sure I wouldn't be afraid of them, if you don't mind them, Gillian!'

'No, you mustn't come,' said the children, and they went off out of the front gate with Bobs trotting beside them.

'I *will* go!' thought Bimbo, and he ran to the hedge that grew round the front garden.

'I'm not afraid of dogs or of cars either! I'll join the children and Bobs when they come by – and how surprised they will be to see me trotting with them too!'

So when Bobs and the children came by on the pavement near the hedge, Bimbo crept out and ran behind them. Pad-pad-pad, his feet went, pad-pad-pad. Bobs turned round and looked at him.

'You naughty kitten!' said Bobs. 'You heard what the children said. Go home.'

'I shan't,' said Bimbo. 'I want to go for a walk just as you do. I'm a big kitten now.'

Just then a car raced by and Bimbo meowed in fright. 'Oh, what's that enormous thing? Oh, it's shouting at me. I don't like it! Bobs, Bobs, will it eat me?'

'Bimbo, that's only a car hooting,' said Bobs. 'Of course it won't eat you.'

'There's another one!' cried Bimbo. 'Oh, suppose it comes on the pavement and gobbles me up? Bobs, I know those big things would eat me for their dinner.'

'No, they wouldn't,' said Bobs. 'They don't have any dinner. Don't be silly.'

Suddenly a dog came by, and was most surprised to see a kitten out for a walk. 'Wuff!'

he barked. 'Look what's here to chase! Run, kitten, run, I'm going to come after you!'

'You're not to!' mewed Bimbo, and ran between Bobs' legs. 'Save me, Bobs, save me!'

'You're tripping me up!' cried Bobs. And down he went on to the pavement with a bump. The children looked round to see what the matter was – and how surprised they were to see naughty Bimbo tearing down the pavement as fast as his brown legs would take him – with a dog after him, barking madly!

'Where's the gate, oh, where's the gate?' panted Bimbo. 'I can't see it! I've passed it! I must climb a tree!'

So up a tree went the kitten, and was very glad that the dog couldn't climb it too. The dog sat down at the foot, his tongue hanging out.

'I'll wait till you come down,' he said. 'You're good to chase!'

So there poor Bimbo had to stay till the children came back from their walk and saw him.

'Oh, look! There's poor Bimbo up the tree!' said Gillian in surprise. 'Go away, dog!

Bimbo, jump on to my shoulder!'

So down Bimbo jumped and landed safely on Gillian's shoulder. The dog ran away.

'I'll watch for you to go walking again,' he wuffed. 'Then we'll have another race!'

But Bimbo had had enough of going for walks! '*You* can go out each day for a walk, Bobs,' he said, 'and so can Gillian and Imogen. But I shan't. Walks are dangerous for kittens like me!'

'Well, isn't that exactly what I told you?' wuffed Bobs. 'You just be sensible – or I'll chase you myself!'

Chapter 2
A Playmate for Bimbo

Bimbo wanted somebody to play with. Bobs didn't always want to play. Cosy didn't mind sometimes, but if Bimbo was rough, she smacked him hard with her paw and he didn't like that.

Gillian and Imogen went to school. So there wasn't really anyone for him to play with.

'I wish I had someone to play with!' he kept sighing. 'I do wish I had. Somebody silly like myself, who will play chase-my-tail and hide-under-the-bed, and skip-around, and pounce-at-your-feet. Those are the games I love. But nobody will play them with me.'

And then one day a playmate came for Bimbo. She came in a big basket, much bigger than the one Bimbo had come in. She arrived at the station in this basket, and she was fetched in the car. The basket was put down in the nursery, and the two children looked at it excitedly.

'Somebody nice is in here,' said Mummy, and she undid the strap.

'Who?' asked Gillian. 'Do tell us! Is it somebody for us?'

'Yes, for you,' said Mummy. 'Somebody to live in the nursery and belong to you. It's a little puppy called Topsy!'

Up went the lid – but nobody jumped out. The children and Mummy looked inside. There, on some straw, lay a small white fox-terrier dog, with a pretty black head and black tail. She looked up at the three people with soft brown eyes. She was frightened.

'Hello, Topsy!' said Gillian, in a gentle voice. 'Don't be frightened! You've come to a good home, and we will love you and be kind to you. Jump out and let us have a look at you.'

Topsy stood up. She was a dear little puppy about five months old. She wagged her tail just a little. It was a signal to say that she wanted to be friends.

'You poor little frightened thing!' said Imogen. 'I expect you can't understand being sent away from your mother and your home. This must seem very strange to you. Never mind – you will soon know us and get used to us. We will love you very much, and you will love us.'

Gillian lifted the puppy out of the big basket. Imogen put down a plate of biscuits and milk. The puppy smelt them and ran to the plate. Soon she was eating greedily.

Then she went to Gillian and tried to jump on to her lap. Gillian let her cuddle there, and she licked her hands.

'Oh, let me have a turn at having Topsy on my knee too,' said Imogen, who loved cuddling toys and animals. So Topsy had a turn at cuddling on Imogen's knee, and she soon began to think that she had come to a very nice new home!

And then Bimbo came running into the nursery to see what all the fuss was about! He stopped when he saw Topsy. What was this – was it Bobs gone a bit small?

Then he smelt a different smell – not Bobs' smell. It must be a new dog, a small one.

Topsy jumped down and sniffed at Bimbo's nose. Bimbo hissed a little, for he wasn't quite certain if this was the kind of dog who might suddenly chase him.

Topsy wagged the tip of her tail very slightly. Bobs had already told Bimbo that a dog's tail was used as a signal for friendship. If a dog wants to be friendly he wags his tail – so Bimbo stopped hissing when he saw that, and sniffed round Topsy's mouth, smelling the biscuit and milk she had eaten.

Topsy wagged her tail in delight. To and fro it went, to and fro, as if it was on a spring.

Then she gave a little yap and ran all round Bimbo.

'Play with me! I'm sure you are not a grown-up cat! I'm not a grown-up dog either. I'm a puppy-dog. Are you a puppy-cat?'

'No, I'm a kitten-cat,' said Bimbo, and he crouched down behind a chair-leg, ready to jump out at Topsy. 'Catch me if you can!'

And then began such a chase round the nursery, in and out of the chairs, round the piano, over the doll's house and under the table!

'Oh, look – they *have* made friends quick-ly!' cried Gillian. 'Aren't they funny!'

Bimbo squeezed inside the toy cupboard and Topsy couldn't imagine where he had gone. Then she smelt the kitten in the cup-board and got inside too. What a scramble round there was! Out flew the small teddy bear – plop! Out flew the clockwork mouse and his key dropped out – ping! Out came half a dozen wooden skittles – clitter-clatter, clitter-clatter!

'Hey! This won't do!' cried Gillian. 'Come out, you scamps! We don't want the whole of the toy cupboard turned out. It's not spring-cleaning time yet!'

The two animals jumped out. Topsy shook herself and sat down, panting, with her tongue hanging out, nice and pink. Bimbo sat down beside her and began to wash himself all over – lick-lick-lick.

'What are you licking yourself for?' asked Topsy. 'Do you taste sweet?'

'Ha, ha, funny joke!' said Bimbo, and went on cleaning himself. 'Topsy, I like you. I'm sure you've been brought here to play with me and have fun. Let's be good friends, shall we?'

'Wuff-wuff, of course we will!' said Topsy, and wagged her tail so hard that it looked like two or three tails wagging at once!

Chapter 3
Topsy Makes a Mistake

The cook didn't like Topsy or Bimbo in her kitchen. 'Now you just go out!' she said to Bimbo. 'I know quite well that as soon as my back is turned you'll be up on the kitchen table after my sausages.'

She shook her rolling-pin at Bimbo and he fled. Topsy looked up at the cook with her soft brown eyes.

'It's no good you looking at me like that,' said the cook. 'You're just as bad. I daresay you won't jump up on the table – but you'll get under my feet all the time, and trip me up. Be off with you!'

Topsy ran out of the kitchen to find Bimbo. 'Isn't it a pity we can't go into the kitchen whenever we want to?' said Topsy. 'It does smell so nice. I like it better than any room in the house, because of its delicious smell.'

'Oh, I know another room that's much nicer,' said Bimbo. 'It's a wonderful room, where meals are always set out ready on shelves – but nobody goes to eat them there; it does seem such a waste.'

'Bones and biscuits, what room's that?' asked Topsy, in the greatest surprise. '*I* don't know it.'

'Well, I'll take you to it,' said Bimbo. 'But you'll find the door is shut. I wish I knew who the meals are waiting for, in that nice little room. I've never seen anyone taken there. If the cook goes there she always shoos me away before she opens the door. But I've seen and smelt all the delicious things through the open door!'

When the cook was out that afternoon Bimbo took Topsy down the stairs and into the kitchen. He showed her a door. 'The room's behind that door,' said Bimbo. 'Topsy, put your nose to the crack, and sniff. Isn't it delicious?'

Topsy put her nose to the door.

'Tails and whiskers!' she said. 'What a

glorious smell! I can smell meat – and fish –
and pie – and sardines left over from breakfast – and bones!'

'Look out! Here comes somebody!' hissed
Bimbo. Topsy ran under the big kitchen
chair and hid there. Bimbo lay down on the
hearthrug. Gillian came into the kitchen and
went to the larder door, under which the two
animals had been so busily sniffing.

She opened it and took out the cake-tin
from the corner. She carried the tin to the
kitchen table and took off the lid. Bimbo got

up slyly and slipped quietly round the side of the open larder door. Topsy saw him and slipped round too.

Gillian was humming a song to herself and didn't hear or see either of them. She took out the cake for tea and put the tin back into its corner of the larder again. Then she ran upstairs with the cake on a plate – but first she shut the larder door!

And she shut in Bimbo and Topsy of course! But they didn't mind. They didn't mind a bit. They were pleased. It was a nice little room to be shut inside. Oh, the smells there!

'What did I tell you?' said Bimbo to Topsy. 'Look at that big meal on the shelf there! Who's it for? Nobody comes to eat here. It's all wasted, it seems to me. Well – it won't be wasted now. Up I go!'

And up on the first shelf Bimbo went. Topsy put her front paws up on the shelf, but she couldn't jump on it as Bimbo did. It was most annoying.

'I'll push you something off,' said Bimbo. 'Just tell me what you'd like. Do you fancy a joint of meat? It's not cooked, so it smells very good indeed. Or there are a few herrings here. And what's this – a rabbit! Oh Topsy, would you like a rabbit? It's cooked.'

'Yes. I'd like a rabbit more than anything,' said Topsy, jumping up and down eagerly. 'Push it over. And push over the meat too. Hurry, for I'm so hungry I can't wait!'

Crash! Over the edge of the shelf went the big brown pot in which the rabbit had been cooked. It tipped over and the gravy ran out. Joints of rabbit fell out and Topsy got her sharp teeth into them at once. Crunch, crunch! Oh, how marvellous!

'What are *you* having?' she called up to Bimbo.

'I've found a jug of yellow custard,' said Bimbo. 'And some sardines. Wait a minute – I'll send over a sardine or two – and I'll tip up the jug to drip a little custard on to the floor.'

Drip-drip – down came some custard on Topsy's head, and two sardines. What a feast the puppy had!

'You know, Bimbo, I really think this meal must have been laid for us,' said Topsy, try-ing to lick the custard off her left ear with her tongue. 'There are all the things we like.'

Just then they heard Gillian's voice calling loudly. 'Topsy, Topsy, Tops! Topsy, Topsy, Tops! Where are you? Where *can* that dog have gone to? And where's Bimbo? Bim-bim-bim-bimbo!'

'Oh, Gillian is going for a walk!' said Topsy. 'Oh, I *must* go with her, I simply must.'

'Why must you?' asked Bimbo, chewing the head off a herring.

'Well, because there are so many glorious smells all along the lane,' said Topsy, scratching at the door. 'I simply love to smell them every day.'

'Topsy, Topsy, Topsy!' shouted Gillian. Topsy whined loudly, and Bimbo was cross.

'Don't make that noise! We aren't supposed to be here, and if anyone hears us we shall get into dreadful trouble.'

'Why shall we?' said Topsy. 'I'm sure this meal was meant for us! Oh, I do hope Gillian won't go without me.'

But she did – and Topsy was so unhappy about it that she wouldn't eat anything more at all, not even when Bimbo emptied a jug of milk over her and told her to lick it up.

The cook came back after tea. When she

came into the kitchen she stared in amazement at the larder door. From underneath it came a stream of custard, milk and rabbit gravy. How very peculiar!

She opened the door – and out shot a very cross Topsy and a frightened Bimbo. 'Oh, you wicked creatures!' cried the cook, when she saw the mess her larder was in! 'What will your mistress say to you! How did you get in? The door was shut! You couldn't have squeezed under the door or got in through the keyhole. It's a real puzzle!'

When Mistress heard what had happened she was very cross indeed. 'You must both be scolded,' she said. 'Bimbo, you know quite well that cats are not allowed in the larder. Topsy, you mustn't believe all that naughty Bimbo tells you. Come here!'

Scold-scold-scold! Poor Topsy. Poor Bimbo. Topsy crept to her basket and lay down with her ears drooping and her tail between her legs. Bimbo fled away to the nursery and hid at the back of the toy cupboard. He was very angry.

'I'll tell Gillian all about it when she comes in!' he said. So he did – but Gillian put on a very stern face and shook her head. 'You're naughty and mischievous. Larders aren't for puppies or kittens. You know that very well! I am ashamed of you both.'

'We'll never go into the larder again!' whined Topsy.

'Never, never!' mewed Bimbo. So they were forgiven, and before very long Topsy was curled up on Gillian's knee, dreaming of rabbit and custard, and Bimbo was cuddled on Imogen's knee, dreaming of milk and herring.

And Cosy, the tabby-cat, licked up all the rabbit gravy, the milk and the custard from the floor and had a perfectly lovely time.

'She might have said "Thank you" to us!' said Topsy.

But she didn't!

Chapter 4
Bimbo Gets a Shock

Topsy and Bobs, the two dogs, often used to get baths when they were dirty. How they hated that! As soon as Bobs saw the bath being dragged out of the shed, he ran away out of the front gate. So Gillian had to catch him first, and tie him up – and then get the bath out.

Topsy didn't know what the bath was at first. When she heard Gillian pulling it out of the shed – clank-clank-clank – she ran to see whatever could be making the noise.

Bobs was tied up near by. He growled at Topsy. 'It's all because of *you* that we're going to have baths,' he said. 'You rolled in the mud this morning, and Mistress said, "Topsy does smell! She must have a bath – so

31

Bobs may as well have one too, though he's not really dirty." I do feel cross with you, Topsy.'

'Why, what's the matter with a bath?' said Topsy, surprised. 'This thing is a bath, isn't it? Well, what harm can it do us?'

'You wait and see!' said Bobs. So Topsy waited – and when the bath was filled with water, what a surprise she got! Gillian lifted her up and put her, splash, into the big bath. And then Imogen soaped her well.

'Don't wriggle so,' said Imogen, 'or the soap will get into your eyes.'

But Topsy did wriggle, and the soap did get into her eyes. How she howled! Imogen poured some water over her head to get the soap out. Topsy didn't like that either. She didn't like the hot water, she didn't like the soap, she didn't like being wet, and she didn't like being rubbed dry. She didn't like anything about the bath at all.

'Now you see what I mean when I say that baths are horrid,' said Bobs, trying to pull away from the rope that tied him to a railing near by. 'You've had your turn – now mine is coming, and I'm not really dirty, either!'

'Will Bimbo have his turn after you?' asked Topsy, shaking hundreds of drops from her wet coat.

'Don't do that all over me,' said Bobs, 'I shall have enough water on me in a minute without you wetting me too! Of course Bimbo won't have a bath, silly. Cats never do.'

'Well, I don't call that fair!' said Topsy angrily. 'Why should dogs have to have baths, when cats never do? I'm sure Bimbo gets just as dirty as I do.'

Bimbo ran up joyfully when he saw the bath steaming in the garden. 'Ha ha!' he mewed. 'A bath! I see you've had one, Topsy! How did you like it? What dirty creatures dogs must be, always having baths. I'll sit and watch Bobs having his.'

'No, you won't,' said Bobs. 'You just go away. I'm not going to have you sitting there grinning whenever I get soap in my eyes.'

But Bobs had to have his bath with Bimbo sitting there. How that kitten laughed when Bobs yelped that the water was too hot! How he enjoyed it when Bobs whined because he got the soap in his eyes!

'Topsy, how can you stand there and let Bimbo laugh at me like that!' cried Bobs. 'Chase him away.'

So Topsy ran at Bimbo. At first Bimbo just rolled over to play with her, but when he found that Topsy gave him a nip on his tail to make him run, he ran! He wasn't going to have his fine long tail nipped like that.

Bimbo tore down the garden. Topsy chased after him, yapping at his heels. Bimbo leapt over the wall, and disappeared. But Topsy found a hole to squeeze through and soon Bimbo found her after him again.

The kitten tore back to the wall that ran at the bottom of his own garden, and jumped up on it. Topsy jumped to see if she could get Bimbo's tail – and the kitten leapt down on the other side in a great hurry. Off he went up the garden again.

He ran all round the house with Topsy after him, and then jumped up on to the roof of the shed. He lost his balance – and fell.

And, oh dear me, just under the shed was the bath! Gillian had pulled it over there to empty it down the drain. She was just tipping it up – and Bimbo fell right into it.

SPLASH! Gillian was so surprised to see Bimbo in the bath. But Bimbo was even more surprised. Ooooh! Water! How horrible, how frightening!

'Bimbo wants a bath!' cried Imogen in delight. 'He's jumped into the water. Let me soap him.'

And before poor Bimbo could do anything about it, there was Imogen soaping him for all she was worth. Bimbo wriggled and mewed, and the soap went into his eyes. Then how he yowled!

'Wuff, wuff, wuff!' laughed Bobs and Topsy. 'This is a great joke! Bimbo laughed at us for having a bath – and now he's having a bath too! Is the water nice and wet, Bimmy? Is the soap slippery? Are you clean?'

Bimbo put out his claws and Imogen let go. She didn't want to be scratched!

Bimbo jumped out of the water. He mewed and shook himself. Showers of drops flew everywhere. Gillian threw a towel over him and began to rub him dry. But Bimbo did not want to be rubbed, and he shot off down the garden with the towel trailing behind.

How the two dogs laughed! 'Did you like your bath, Bimbo?' they cried. 'Was it lovely? You won't sit and laugh at us next time, will you?'

And Bimbo certainly won't! As soon as he sees that bath being dragged out of the shed, he's off to the bottom of the next-garden-but-one. No more baths for Bimbo!

Chapter 5
Topsy Wants a New Tail

Topsy didn't like her tail very much. She thought it was much too short. She liked Bimbo's long brown tail very much indeed.

'I wish I had a long tail like yours,' she said. 'Bones and biscuits, couldn't I wag it beautifully then!'

'It *is* nice to wave a long tail about,' said Bimbo. 'But I like to wave mine to and fro when I'm cross, Topsy, not when I'm friendly, like you.'

'Yes, I've noticed that,' said Topsy. 'If I had a long tail I wouldn't waste it on cross waggings. I'd have a marvellous time shaking it at every dog I met!'

'Well, I'm sorry I can't lend you my tail,'

said Bimbo. 'It's a pity dogs have such short, ugly tails. Yours isn't much more than a stump!'

Bimbo thought quite a lot about Topsy and her tail. He wished he could get her a nice long one. And then one day he heard Gillian say something that made him feel quite excited.

Gillian was talking to Imogen. She had a book on her knee and she said, 'You know, Imogen, this book has the most lovely tales in it. You ought to read it.'

'What sort of tales?' asked Imogen. 'Long tales or short tales?'

'It's got both,' said Gillian. 'Look, I'll put the book back into the bookshelf, Imogen, and you can get it when you want a nice long tale.'

Well, when Bimbo heard that, his whiskers shook with excitement. So that was where long tails were kept – in books! How marvellous – now he might be able to get one for Topsy to wear.

He ran off to find the puppy. She was sitting by the gardener, watching him dig in the earth.

'Hello!' said Topsy. 'The gardener is aw-

fully busy digging this morning. I think there must be hidden treasure somewhere here, because he's digging and digging. I'm waiting for him to find it.'

'Well, you'll wait for weeks then,' said Bimbo. 'He's only digging a trench for seeds! Listen, Topsy, I've heard something lovely this morning.'

'What?' asked Topsy. 'Are we going to have something special for dinner – or is Gillian going to take me for a long walk?'

'No – something much better than that!'

said Bimbo. 'I know where we can find a long tail for you!'

'Bones and biscuits!' said Topsy in delight. 'That's good news! Where's the tail? Do we have to buy it?'

'Oh no – we can find one in the nursery,' said Bimbo. 'I heard Gillian say so. They are kept inside those things called books. Gillian said there were long tails and short tails there. We'll find the longest one there is and get it for you. Then you'll have a lovely time waving it about!'

'Fine!' said Topsy, jumping up and down and setting her tail going wag-wag-wag. 'Come on – let's go and get it.'

Off they went up the garden and into the house. They rushed up to the nursery. There was no one there. The children had gone to school.

'In that book shelf there must be hundreds of tails,' said Bimbo, looking at all the story books there. 'Hundreds and hundreds.'

'Well, hurry up and find a few for me to try on!' said Topsy, prancing round in excitement. 'Where are they? I can't see any sticking out.'

'Wait a minute, Topsy – what are we going

to do about the tail you're wearing now?'
said Bimbo suddenly. 'You can't wear two
tails, you know.'

'Can't we find a black tail to match mine,
and tie it on?' said Topsy. 'I don't want you
to cut mine off. I shouldn't like that at all.'

'All right,' said Bimbo. 'We'll try to find a
nice long wavy black tail! Come on! Pull out
two or three of these books and hunt for tails
inside them.'

So before two minutes had gone by, there
was a marvellous mess on the floor! Books of
all kinds had been pulled out, and opened.
Bimbo and Topsy sniffed and sniffed at the
pages – but to their great disappointment,
not a single tail could they find!

'Well, that's funny,' said Bimbo, sitting down and beginning to wash himself. 'I know I heard Gillian say there were long and short tails in these books – and especially in *this* book, because she had it on her knee whilst she spoke.'

'I do so want a long tail,' whined Topsy, sniffing round the books. She took hold of a page with her sharp little puppy teeth, and tore it out. But still there wasn't a tail to be found! So she tore out a few more pages just because she was cross!

And then Bobs came trotting into the room. How he stared when he saw the mess on the floor!

'Whatever are you doing?' he said. 'You *will* get into trouble!'

'We're trying to find a long tail for Topsy,' said Bimbo. 'That's all.'

'Well, you won't find one in those books,' said Bobs. 'I should have thought anyone would have known that!'

Bimbo explained what he had heard Gillian say – and then how Bobs laughed! He laughed and he laughed, and Bimbo and Topsy saw all his strong white teeth and pink tongue.

'Whatever are you laughing at?' said Bimbo in surprise. 'Have we said anything funny?'

'Bimbo, the tales in books are meant to be *read* and not worn or wagged!' said Bobs, beginning to laugh all over again. 'They're not furry tails like ours – they are made of words that go on and on over the pages. Oh, what a silly pair you are!'

Just then the children came home from school, and Bobs disappeared.

'I'm not going to be blamed for that mess on the floor,' he said. 'Goodbye – and I expect you'll have a fine tale to tell me when you see me next – but you won't wag it!'

Poor Bimbo and Topsy. They had a sad tale to tell Bobs that evening.

'We got dreadfully scolded,' said Bimbo. 'I feel very unhappy.'

Bobs looked at Topsy. 'I see you've even lost what tail you had!' he said. Topsy looked round to the back of her. Her tail wasn't there! Not a tail, not a wag was to be seen. She was most alarmed.

'Oh, Bimbo, even my little short tail is gone!' she wuffed. 'What can have happened to it? It's usually sticking up straight at the

end of me, ready to wag and wag. But it isn't
there!'

Bimbo looked. Sure enough there was no
nice little stump of tail there. Topsy looked
so funny without it.

'You've dropped it somewhere, I suppose,'
said Bimbo. 'Oh, what a pity! Well, we'd better look for it before it gets swept up and put
into the dustbin.'

'I don't want my tail put into the dustbin,'
wept poor Topsy. 'It was only a short one, but
I liked it. It was so waggy. Oh, wherever can it
be?'

Bobs laughed. He wouldn't join in the

hunt. He lay with his nose on his paws and watched the puppy and the kitten sniff all round for the lost tail. They hunted under the couch. They looked under every chair. They sniffed down the passageway. They looked under every cushion.

'It's gone,' said Topsy. 'Perhaps Cosy came in and found it and chewed it up. Oh dear, oh dear – Gillian and Imogen won't like me any more without a tail. What an unlucky day this is! We look for a new tail for me and don't find one – and then I go and lose my old tail too!'

Gillian and Imogen came running into the room. 'Come for a walk, Topsy!' they cried. Topsy jumped up in delight. And Bimbo gave a loud meow of surprise.

'Topsy! Your tail is back. Look, look!'

Sure enough there was Topsy's little tail wagging hard. How strange!

'But where was it?' barked Topsy.

Then Bobs laughed and said: 'It was on the back of you all the time, Topsy! But you had been scolded and you were sad – so your tail went right down between your back legs – and you couldn't see it! But as soon as Gillian said "walk" you felt happy and your tail sprang up again to wag! Oh, what a funny dog you are!'

'Hurray! I'm happy again!' cried Topsy. 'I've got my waggy tail – and I shall keep it now and not go hunting all over the place for a new one! Come on, Gillian – I'm ready for a walk!'

And off went the children and Topsy – and you should have seen her tail! Wag-wag-wag, it went, wag-wag-wag! I'm a happy tail on a happy dog. Wag-wag-wag!

Chapter 6
Bimbo Disappears

One day Topsy felt as if she must tease Bobs, Cosy and Bimbo. She even felt that she must tease the white pigeons on the lawn.

So every time the pigeons flew down she ran at them and sent them away into the air again, with a great flapping of wings.

Then she saw Cosy asleep on the wall, with her striped tail hanging down. Topsy jumped up at the tail and nipped it hard. Cosy awoke with a yowl, leapt high into the air and disappeared over the wall into the next garden.

Topsy thought this was great fun. She felt sure that Bobs was asleep somewhere. What about teasing him too? So she hunted around for Bobs, and at last found him. He was lying fast asleep in the shade of a bush, for it was a hot day.

Topsy crept up to Bobs. She came over the grass, and her little feet didn't make any sound at all. She crept nearer – and nearer – and nearer.

Then, with a yelp and a bound, she pounced right on to Bobs, jumping on to his middle!

He awoke, and sprang to his four feet in horror, thinking that a hundred elephants at least must have trodden on him. When he saw it was Topsy, he was very angry. He rushed at her and snapped hard with his teeth. Topsy felt her left ear nipped, and gave a yelp. She put her tail down and ran away.

'I shan't go near Bobs again,' she thought. 'He is too fierce.'

So she went to find Bimbo. She soon found him. He was asleep too, for he had spent the night hunting mice in the garden, and he was very sleepy. So there he was, his nose almost hidden in his paws, lying on the sunny seat at the bottom of the garden.

Bimbo's tail hung down just as Cosy's had done.

Topsy crept up. She blew at the tail, and Bimbo curled it up on the seat beside him. But soon it fell down again. Then Topsy nibbled at it as if it were her rubber bone. Nibble-nibble-nibble! Nibble-nibble-nibble!

Bimbo didn't like it. He half woke up, curled up his tail again and went to sleep. Topsy waited till the tail fell down again and began to nibble once more.

That woke Bimbo right up, and he was angry when he saw Topsy sitting near by looking very innocent indeed, as if she didn't know anything about tails or about nibbling them either!'

'Leave me alone!' said Bimbo. 'I know you were fidgeting with my tail, and I don't like it. Let me sleep in peace.'

But as soon as Bimbo went to sleep again Topsy began to tease him. She tickled his nose. She blew down his fluffy ears. She tried to nibble his tail again. So in the end Bimbo jumped off the seat and ran away to find a better place to sleep in. Topsy ran after him.

'I'll find you again, wherever you go!' she wuffed. 'I'm having such fun this morning, teasing everybody!'

Bimbo ran round the house. Topsy went after him – but Bimbo could run faster, and when Topsy turned the corner, Bimbo was gone.

Topsy ran round a little, sniffing hard. But she couldn't find Bimbo anywhere. Gillian came out in a little while with Imogen. 'Hello, Topsy!' said Imogen. 'What are you sniffing round for? Do you want to come for a walk? I'm going out with my dolls' pram. My dolls have been out here in the pram all morning, and now they want a walk.'

But for once Topsy didn't want to go for a

walk. She wanted to find Bimbo. So she ran off down the garden, and Imogen went off with Gillian, wheeling her dolls' pram.

Topsy hunted for Bimbo again. Soon she heard the cook calling! 'Bim-Bim-Bimbo! Dinner! Dinner! Co-co-cosy! Dinner for you, dinner! Nice fish! Come along. Bim-Bim-Bimbo!'

Cosy appeared and ran to the kitchen door. Bobs wandered up, but the cook shooed him off.

'No,' she said, 'you and Topsy have had your dinners. This is for Cosy and Bimbo. Now where is Bimbo? Cosy will eat all this up if Bimbo doesn't hurry up.'

Topsy looked at the fine-smelling fish on the plate. 'If I find Bimbo and tell him his dinner is ready, maybe he will be pleased with me and give me a bit,' she said to herself.

So she went off again to find Bimbo. She looked simply everywhere, and barked loudly for the kitten to come.

'Bimbo! Fish for dinner! Bimbo!' she wuffed. 'Cosy is eating it all. What a silly kitten you are! Dinner, Bimbo, dinner!'

But Bimbo didn't come. It was most mysterious. After a while even Bobs began to be worried. 'Do you suppose anything has happened to Bimbo?' he said to Topsy. 'He *always* comes when he is called, especially if it's for his dinner. I'm really rather worried.'

So then Bobs began to hunt too, in all the places he knew. But Bimbo was gone. He just wasn't anywhere at all. So Cosy ate up all the dinner, and then licked the plate. There was none left for poor Bimbo.

'We must tell Gillian and Imogen when they come home that dear old Bimbo is gone,' said Bobs sadly. 'Won't they be sad? But maybe they can ring up the police and tell them about Bimbo. Someone may have found him and taken him there.'

'I do wish I hadn't teased Bimbo this morning,' said Topsy. 'I feel very bad about it now.'

'Well, I hope you feel as bad about teasing *me*!' said Bobs. 'You are a perfect nuisance sometimes, Topsy. Oh, look – here are the children coming back from their walk! Let's go and tell them the sad news.'

So up they ran and told the news to Gillian and Imogen. But somehow or other the children did not seem at all worried!

'Aren't you sad and sorry?' said Topsy, in surprise. 'You love Bimbo, don't you? Well, why do you smile when we tell you he has quite disappeared?'

'Well, we are smiling because we happen to know where he is!' said Gillian, with a laugh.

'Where?' cried Bobs and Topsy together.

'Show them, Imogen,' said Gillian. So Imogen lifted up the cover of her dolls' pram – and there, curled up with Angela the doll, lay Bimbo, his tail round him, fast asleep!

'Bones and biscuits!' cried Bobs. 'Whoever would have thought of a hiding-place like that! Did you take him out for a walk, Imogen?'

'Yes,' said Imogen. 'You see, I didn't know he was in the pram – and off I went, pushing it, thinking that Angela was really rather heavy today.'

'And suddenly,' said Gillian, 'quite suddenly we saw something moving a little under the pram rug. Imogen was so surprised. She said, "Oh, Gillian. I believe Angela is kicking her legs about. Isn't it strange?"'

'And then I looked under the pram rug to see, and I saw Bimbo curled up there, fast asleep,' said Imogen, with a laugh. 'I did get such a surprise. So we took him for a long walk with Angela and he didn't wake up at all. He's so sleepy, the darling!'

'And to think we've hunted and hunted all over the place for him!' cried Bobs, quite cross. 'We've run for miles all round and round the garden. And Cosy has eaten all his dinner.'

When Bimbo heard the word 'dinner' he woke up at once. He sat up, and looked down in surprise at Angela the doll. Then he remembered how he had got into the pram to hide from Topsy. He looked over the side at the two dogs.

'Well, you didn't find me!' he said wagging his whiskers a little. 'What's this I hear about dinner?'

'Cosy has eaten all yours,' said Topsy. 'Every bit. And licked the plate too. That's what comes of going off in a dolls' pram, silly!'

'Well, I like that!' said Bimbo, jumping out. 'Who teased me and made me hide in a pram? It's all your fault that I was taken off for a walk and didn't know about my dinner. I'll never speak to you again, Topsy!'

And Bimbo stalked indoors, with his tail held straight up in the air, looking as haughty as could be.

Topsy was very upset. She ran after him.

'Bimbo! Don't be cross! I'm sorry.'

'No, you're not,' said Bimbo. 'I know you! You're a horrid, teasing puppy-dog, and I don't know why I liked you. I shall never like you again. Don't dare to speak to me!'

And no matter what poor Topsy tried to say or do to Bimbo, he wouldn't even look at her. He wouldn't speak to her or play with her.

'What shall I do about it, Bobs?' said Topsy sadly. 'Bimbo is my very best friend. It is dreadful to quarrel like this.'

'Well, you must put it right,' said Bobs. 'You made him lose his dinner – why not give him your supper, when it comes? Maybe he won't feel so angry with you then.'

'That's a good idea,' said Topsy, cheering up a little. So when Mistress put down her supper, she didn't gobble it up, but only just sniffed at it.

'Tails and whiskers – it's such a nice supper,' groaned Topsy. 'Mince and gravy and biscuits all mixed up together. Oh my!'

But Topsy didn't touch it. Instead she ran to where Bimbo was curled up in front of the nursery fire.

'Bimbo!' she said.

'Be quiet and go away,' hissed Bimbo. 'I feel like scratching tonight, so be careful.'

'Bimbo, I've got something for you,' said Topsy.

'Yes – a few more nibbles, I suppose,' said

Bimbo. 'Well, I've got about a hundred scratches in my claws. Just come a bit nearer and you shall feel them.'

'Bimbo – I *have* got a few nibbles for you,' said Topsy. 'But not the kind you mean! My supper is down in the kitchen – you can have it all for yourself. It is mince and gravy and biscuits!'

'Oh, Topsy – do you mean that?' said Bimbo, jumping to his feet at once. 'Where is it? Quick, take me to it – I'm so hungry I could almost eat the plate too.'

'No, don't do that, or the cook will be cross,' said Topsy. 'Come on, before Bobs finds it and gobbles it up.'

So downstairs they went – and before ten minutes had passed that supper was all eaten by Bimbo. He chewed the mince carefully. He crunched up the biscuits. He licked up the gravy.

'How slowly you eat!' said Topsy, with a sigh. 'I could have gobbled that all up in half a minute! Did you enjoy it, Bimbo? Will you be friends now?'

'Yes, of course,' said Bimbo, beginning to wash his whiskers carefully. 'Look, Topsy – I've left the plate for you to lick. There is still a little gravy on it.'

So Topsy licked the plate quite clean, and enjoyed it. Bimbo washed himself all over and then strolled upstairs again. Topsy's basket was there. Bimbo jumped into it and curled himself up there.

'Where am I to sleep?' said Topsy. 'That's not a very friendly thing to do, to take my basket, Bimbo. I thought we were going to be friends again.'

'So we are,' said Bimbo, making room for Topsy beside him. 'We are going to sleep in the same basket! I can't be friendlier than that, can I? When a kitten and puppy curl up together, that shows they are the best of friends.'

'Woof!' said Topsy, in delight, and jumped into the basket beside Bimbo. Soon they were curled up together, fast asleep.

And when Gillian and Imogen came into the nursery, how they smiled. 'Look!' said Imogen, 'what friends they are! I'm sure they never, ever quarrel.'

But she wasn't quite right, was she?

Chapter 7
Bimbo and the Trees

Bimbo didn't like any dogs except Bobs and Topsy. He was used to them, but he couldn't bear it if a visitor brought a dog that he didn't know into the house.

'Strange dogs are horrid,' said Bimbo to Topsy. 'I can't think how you can go and wag your tail at them as you do, and sniff at them, and play with them. Horrid, barking things!'

'Don't you like our barks?' asked Topsy in surprise. 'How funny of you! I think a bark is a fine noise. Wuff-wuff-wuff!'

'Don't do that right in my ear!' said Bimbo crossly. 'That's the only thing I don't like about you, Topsy – your horrid, loud bark!'

'Look – here's a visitor coming into the

room – and she's got *two* dogs!' said Topsy, in delight. 'I'll go and make friends with them at once!'

Poor Bimbo! He didn't have any time to rush out of the room, so he had to jump on the top of the piano and hide behind a vase of flowers. He was so afraid of strange dogs that barked.

The two little dogs were on a lead. They were young and wanted to play. They pulled at their leads and tried to dance round Topsy, whose tail was wagging hard.

'Let them off the lead if you like,' said Mistress to the visitor, when she came into the room. 'The cats are not here, so it will be quite all right.'

She didn't see poor frightened Bimbo hiding behind the flowers on the piano. But as soon as those two dogs were off their leads, they smelt Bimbo at once, and rushed joyfully to the piano. One jumped up on the stool and put his paws on the keys – for the piano was open.

'Tinkle, tinkle, crash!' went the notes on the piano. Bimbo was so scared at the noise that he leapt to the top of the old grandfather clock. The dogs saw him and

ran to the foot of the clock, barking madly.

'Wuff-wuff-wuff! Wuff-wuff-wuff! Oh, isn't this a joke! See the cat on the clock! Wuff-wuff-wuff!'

They had loud barks and Bimbo was frightened almost out of his life. He didn't know what to do. He couldn't jump down, for the barking dogs would get him. And the clock was wobbling a bit and might fall. Then what would happen?

Mistress saw Bimbo. She shooed the dogs out of the room and lifted the frightened kitten down. He leapt out of the window as fast as he could go.

Topsy laughed at him. 'Fancy being frightened of little dogs like that!' she wuffed after him.

'I hate their loud barks!' called back Bimbo. 'That's what frightens me more than anything. I hate anything with a bark.'

Bobs trotted up. 'Did I hear you say that you hate anything with a bark?' he said. 'Well, Bimbo, beware! Do not go near the *trees*!'

'Why not?' said Bimbo, in great astonishment.

'Because every tree has a bark!' said Bobs solemnly.

'Oh, Bobs – you're not telling me the truth,' wailed Bimbo, scared.

'Indeed I am,' said Bobs. 'I always tell the truth. You know that. I tell you, each of the trees you see in the garden has a bark. So beware!'

'Will they bark at me if I go too near them or climb up them?' asked Bimbo. 'They never have, so far.'

'Well, try and see,' said Bobs, with a grin. 'You can always run away if they start barking at you, can't you?'

'Bones and biscuits, I was never frightened of trees before!' sighed poor Bimbo. 'Now I shan't dare to go near them!'

And he didn't. Every time he went into the garden he kept to the middle of the lawn, and Cosy was most astonished. 'What's the matter with you, Bimbo?' she asked. 'Why do you always keep to the middle of the grass?'

'I'm afraid of the trees barking at me,' said Bimbo. 'You'd better be careful too, Cosy. If trees bark, they might bite as well!'

'What in the world are you talking about?' said Cosy in surprise. 'No tree can bark – and certainly not bite. Anyway, *I've* never seen a tree with teeth!'

'Well, Bobs said that all trees have a bark,' said Bimbo.

Then Cosy stood still on the grass and laughed till her whiskers shook. 'Come with me and I'll show you how to treat a tree's bark!' she said. 'Why, Bimbo, I sharpen my claws on the bark of trees!'

Bimbo ran with her to a tree, though he was really afraid of it barking at him. Cosy stood up against the tree and scratched down the trunk with her claws to make them sharp. 'I'm scratching the bark!' she said. 'See, I'm scratching the bark. You do it too, Bimbo!'

So Bimbo did – and when he found that the tree didn't bark or bite, he felt so pleased. 'Bobs is a storyteller,' he said. 'He really is.'

But he wasn't. He told the truth, didn't he? – and Bimbo made such a mistake!

Chapter 8
Fun in the Garden

When the leaves blew down from the trees, Topsy and Bimbo were very surprised.

'What is happening to the leaves?' said Topsy. 'Why are the trees throwing them down? Are they tired of them?'

'Of course not, silly,' said Bobs. 'They do that every year. You should see the garden in a few weeks' time – my word, it will be full of leaves!'

So it was. The trees were almost bare by then, because a hard frost had come one night and loosened thousands of them. Then the wind blew, and down fluttered the leaves one by one.

Topsy jumped up at them. Bimbo chased

them as they flew away in front of him. It was fun.

One morning the kitten and the puppy were delighted to see that there were two big heaps of leaves on the lawn.

'Oooh, look at that!' said Bimbo. 'The leaves have tidied themselves up and put themselves all together on the lawn for us to play with. Topsy, you take that pile, and I'll have this. We'll burrow down into the middle of our piles and wait till Cosy and Bobs come by. Then we'll jump out at them and give them a dreadful fright!'

So Topsy got into one big pile and hid there and Bimbo got into the other. It was nice and rustly down in the leaves. They were soft, and felt warm.

Soon Bobs came trot-trotting by, his tail in the air, looking for Topsy. But she didn't seem to be anywhere. How funny! Bobs was quite sure he had seen her go out into the garden a few minutes before.

He called to Cosy, who was creeping after a bird near the hedge. 'Cosy, come here! Have you seen Topsy or Bimbo!'

'No,' said Cosy, as the bird flew away. 'I was looking for Bimbo. I say, Bobs – I've got such a good idea!'

'What?' said Bobs. 'I don't much like your good ideas – but you can tell me if you like.'

'Well, listen,' said Cosy. 'Let's get inside those piles of leaves and wait till Topsy and Bimbo come by – and then we can jump out at them and give them a terrible fright!'

'That really would be fun!' said Bobs, his tail wagging fast. 'I'll get into this pile, Cosy, and you get into that. Whoooooosh – I'm going to dive in head first!'

And into the pile of leaves went Bobs – and into the other went Cosy! But, of course, Topsy and Bimbo were already hidden there. What a fright they got – and what a fright Bobs and Cosy got when they felt something biting and yapping, scratching and yowling, in the middle of those leaves!

'There's a monster there!' yelped Bobs, and began to fight Topsy.

'There's a tiger here!' cried Cosy, and began to scratch with all her might at Bimbo.

The gardener came by just then, and was most astonished to see hundreds of leaves flying all over the lawn, and to hear yowls and hisses, yaps and mews, coming from the middle of them.

'Those animals!' he said to himself. 'Here I go and sweep up those untidy leaves into two neat piles – and the next time I come by I see them being scattered all over the garden again. I'll teach those mischievous animals to play about like that!'

And he fetched his broom and began to sweep up Bobs, Topsy, Cosy and Bimbo as fast as he could. They simply couldn't imagine what was happening! As soon as they found their legs they were swept right off them again and were sent round and round the lawn at top speed, first one and then another.

'What is it, what is it?' yelped Topsy.

'There's a thing that goes swish-swish-swish behind me all the time!' mewed Bimbo.

The four animals fled as fast as their legs could take them away. They sat under the big lilac bush and licked themselves.

'Was it you in the leaves?' Bobs asked Topsy and Bimbo. 'Oh, what a fright you gave me! And then the gardener gave me a worse fright still! Look – he's sweeping the leaves up again – and I'm sure the wind is getting up. What fun if it blows the leaves all over the lawn! Well – he won't be able to sweep the wind away!'

And sure enough, the wind *did* come – and once more the leaves were flying all over the lawn.

'Serves you right!' barked Topsy to the poor gardener. But she was careful not to go too near him! She didn't want to be swept away again.

Chapter 9
Bimbo Plays a Trick

Once Bimbo was naughty, and Mistress said he must go without his dinner.

'You have sharpened your claws on my best chairs,' said Mistress. 'You have scratched the legs terribly. You know quite well you are not supposed to do that, you naughty kitten-cat!'

Bimbo was sad when he didn't have any dinner. He thought he had better see if he could get some of Cosy's. But Cosy was ready for him and hissed and spat so fiercely that he didn't dare to do anything but lie down a little way off and watch Cosy eat up all her dinner, and then lick the drips off her whiskers.

'Couldn't I clean your whiskers for you?'

said Bimbo. But Cosy said no. So Bimbo wandered off to see if Bobs had got any dinner to spare. Bobs was just eating his meal when Bimbo came up.

'Can I have a little, please?' asked Bimbo. 'I haven't had anything to eat all day.'

'Yes, come and have a bite,' said Bobs – but before Bimbo could even lick a spot of gravy, Bobs had cleaned the plate shiny white!

'You are a gobbler!' said Bimbo, in disgust. 'You'll make yourself ill, one of these days.'

'Only if my meat is bad,' said Bobs cheerfully. 'Dogs always gobble. When we were wild dogs and lived in packs together, we had to eat quickly, for if we didn't the next dog gobbled everything! So I can't get out of my gobbling ways, and it's no use expecting me to.'

'Where's Topsy?' asked Bimbo. 'Is she having her dinner yet?'

'It's just been put down outside,' said Bobs. 'Mistress said that Topsy is an untidy eater and must have her meals out-of-doors until she can learn not to make a mess.'

Bimbo hurried off to see if Topsy had eaten all her dinner. She hadn't. She was just running up to it.

'Hello, Bimbo!' said Topsy. 'Look at my lovely dinner! It's a fine big one, isn't it!'

'Topsy, Bobs has just been telling me that once he made himself ill by gobbling up bad meat,' said Bimbo solemnly. 'There's a nasty smell just here. Maybe it's your dinner that has got bad meat in it.'

'It smells good enough to me,' said Topsy cheerfully, and took a sniff at the plate.

'Be careful, Topsy, be careful!' cried Bimbo, pretending to be frightened. 'I can smell such a horrid smell. I really don't want you to be ill. Let me take a bite at your dinner first and see if it's all right.'

'Well, take a bit then,' said Topsy. So Bimbo took a piece of meat and chewed it slowly, putting it from side to side of his mouth as if he were tasting it carefully. He made such a face that Topsy was quite alarmed.

And then Bimbo rolled over and over and groaned terribly. 'Oh, oh, oh! Ooooooh! I've got such a pain! Oh, that meat must be bad. It really must. Quick, fetch Mistress to me, and tell her to make me better. Oooooooh!'

The last 'ooh' was such a dreadful one that Topsy was frightened. She sped off to find Mistress as fast as she could. And as soon as Topsy was gone, that scamp of a kitten jumped up again as lively as could be and began to eat Topsy's dinner!

'That was a good trick!' thought Bimbo, pleased. 'A very good trick indeed! Bones and biscuits, I must hurry and eat this dinner all up or else Topsy will be back and will catch me. Gobble, gobble, gobble! I've never

eaten so fast in my life! Gobble, gobble, gobble!'

And dear me, it *was* gobble, gobble, gobble! You should just have seen Bimbo greedily taking all the meat and biscuits into his mouth and swallowing them without biting them, just as if he were a dog! It didn't take him long to empty the plate!

Topsy found Mistress. She tugged at her skirt. 'Quick! Quick! Come and see to Bimbo! He ate some bad meat out of my dinner and he's terribly ill. Quick! Quick!'

Mistress hurried out of doors with Topsy. But there was no Bimbo there. How strange! Mistress looked all around and so did Topsy.

'Where is he?' wondered Topsy, puzzled. 'And oh, tails and whiskers, where's my *dinner*!'

There wasn't any dinner. The plate was licked clean. It was all gone. Then Topsy knew what had happened and she gave an angry wuff and flew off to find Bimbo.

And do you know what was happening to that naughty kitten? Well, he had eaten up Topsy's dinner so fast that he had *really* made himself ill! He had a dreadful pain in his middle and was groaning away to himself in a corner. He saw Topsy coming and cried out to her: 'I'm ill, I'm ill! Go and fetch Mistress to make me better!'

But Topsy wasn't going to do that again. 'I've fetched Mistress once!' she cried, 'and I found my nice dinner all eaten up. You're not going to play the same trick twice!'

And she ran at Bimbo and nipped the end of his brown tail. She wouldn't let him come indoors by the warm fire all day long, though poor Bimbo really did have a terrible pain in his middle. But it served him right, didn't it!

He won't eat Topsy's dinner again in a hurry!

Chapter 10
The Little Red Jersey

Mistress was making a little red jersey for Imogen. She had done the back and now she was doing the front. Topsy and Bimbo often watched her knitting needles going clickity-click, clickity-click, as she worked.

'Dear, dear! How careless I am!' said Mistress one morning. 'I've dropped at least three stitches!'

Topsy pricked up her ears. Poor Mistress! 'Never mind!' wuffed Topsy. 'I'll find the stitches you've dropped, Mistress! Come on, Bimbo, help me. They must be somewhere under Mistress's chair, because that's where she has been sitting for some time whilst she knitted.'

Well, Topsy hunted all around, with her little black nose to the ground. But she couldn't find those dropped stitches at all! And Bimbo hunted too, till he was quite tired with looking.

'What *are* you two animals rushing round and round my legs for?' said Mistress at last. 'Anyone would think I've dropped some sardines or something, the way you are nosing round under my chair!'

'Mistress, you didn't drop sardines, but you said you'd dropped some stitches!' barked Topsy. 'We are trying to find them for you.'

Then Mistress laughed and laughed. 'You silly little dog!' she said. 'When people drop stitches in their knitting, they don't drop them on the floor. But all the same, it was very sweet of you to try to find them. Don't worry any more, I have picked them up myself.'

'That's funny,' said Bimbo to Topsy. 'I didn't see Mistress pick up anything, did you?'

'What I'm *really* worried about,' said Mistress, 'is that I don't believe I shall have enough wool to finish this little red jersey! That's really a nuisance!'

She rolled up the knitting and put it into a bag. Then she gave Topsy a pat and Bimbo a stroke and went out of the room.

Cosy came running in. Topsy told her about the jersey. 'Mistress says she won't have enough wool to finish that little jersey,' said Topsy. Cosy looked up at the bag where the knitting was. A strand of red wool was sticking out of it.

'I'd like to see that jersey,' said Cosy. 'Let's get down the bag and take the jersey out.'

So the three animals got down the bag and Topsy pulled out the knitting with her teeth. One of the needles fell out on to the floor. And then another and another.

'Oh dear!' said Cosy. 'We shall never find the right place to put them back. Look, Topsy – here's some loose wool. Do you think Mistress knew she had it?'

Topsy tugged at the wool with her teeth. It was really part of the knitting, but the puppy didn't know it. A very long thread unravelled itself. Topsy was delighted.

'Just look!' she said. 'Here's a beautiful long bit of wool for Mistress!'

'Pull it,' said Bimbo, getting excited. 'This is fun! We'll pull the wool right out and then try and roll it up into a ball for Mistress to use. Maybe she will have enough then to finish the jersey.'

So Topsy pulled. The wool came out in a very long string – more and more and more – it was great fun. Soon it stretched right across the nursery!

'I don't somehow feel as if we are doing a very good thing,' said Cosy.

'Oh, don't be silly!' said Bimbo. 'You've no idea how pleased Mistress will be when she sees all the wool we've found for her. Perhaps she didn't know she'd got all this tucked away in the bag.'

More and more wool came out as the jersey unravelled. The animals got excited about it. Cosy tried to roll it up into a ball, but the more she tried, the worse tangle it got into.

Then Bimbo went mad. He often did when he had string or something like that to play with. He raced round and round the room, getting all tangled up in the strands of wool. They got caught round chair legs. They got wound round the table. Soon the room looked most peculiar indeed!

'I don't feel as if Mistress will like this

much,' said Topsy at last. 'I'm sure we've got enough wool to make into a beautiful big ball for Mistress – quite enough to finish the jersey – but it won't seem to roll up tidily. it keeps getting into a terrible tangle!'

Just then the nursery door opened and in came Gillian. How she stared when she saw all the wool wound round the nursery furniture!

'Mummy!' she called. 'Come in quickly! The animals have got your knitting.'

Mistress came running into the room. 'Good gracious!' she cried. 'The mischievous things! Oh, look – they've pulled the little red jersey all undone. I shall have to begin it all over again. Bad Topsy! Bad Bimbo! Naughty Cosy!'

'Mistress, don't be cross – don't you see what a lovely lot of wool we've found for you!' wuffed Topsy. 'You will be able to finish the jersey now.'

'*Finish* it!' cried Mistress. 'Begin it all over again, you mean! Why, the wool you've found for me is the wool I knitted into the jersey! Now you've pulled it all undone. There's a good scolding coming to all of you, if you just wait a minute!'

But nobody waited. Topsy fled downstairs with her tail between her legs, and hid under the lilac bush. Cosy disappeared over the wall into the next garden. Bimbo climbed up to the top of the shed, where he was quite safe.

And poor Mistress had to spend an hour unwinding the wool from the furniture. You can guess that she didn't feel at all pleased!

Chapter 11
Fur Coats in Summer

It was a very hot day. The sun shone down and the flowers drooped in the heat. The birds came to Topsy's bowl of drinking water, and used it for a bath.

Topsy was cross. 'Do you suppose I want to drink your bath-water!' she said to the birds. 'Go away! Go and bathe in the pond next door!'

But the birds came down to the bowl every time that Topsy wasn't looking, and she got very cross indeed. She chased them away every time, and soon she was panting with the heat.

Her tongue hung out, very pink indeed. Bimbo didn't like it.

'Do put your tongue back into your

mouth,' he said. 'It looks so silly hanging out like that. Are you cooling it, or what?'

'I just can't help it,' said Topsy, putting her tongue back into her mouth again. 'As soon as I pant, out comes my tongue.'

'Well, it's rude to put your tongue out at me like that,' said Bimbo. 'There it goes again! Topsy, put it back!'

Topsy flopped down beside Bimbo. 'I'm so hot,' she said. 'So very hot.'

'So am I,' said Bimbo. 'I wish I could get cool. But I can't.'

'You've got a thicker fur coat than I have,' said Topsy, looking at Bimbo's creamy coat. 'Isn't it silly of us to wear fur coats in the summer, Bimbo?'

'Very silly,' said Bimbo. 'Mistress only wears hers in the winter. She wears a thin cotton frock in this hot weather. Her fur coat is put away in the wardrobe.'

'Why can't we take off our fur coats and put them away somewhere too?' said Topsy suddenly. 'Oh, Bimbo – wouldn't it be nice if we just wore our skins? We'd be so cool!'

'Well, I don't see why we should not,' said Bimbo, quite pleased at the idea. 'I shall melt away if I get much hotter. I know I shall. How does Mistress take off her fur coat, Topsy?'

'I think she undoes hooks or buttons,' said Topsy. 'At least, I've seen hooks and buttons on dresses and coats, so I expect there are some on fur coats too.'

'Then that's how we ought to take ours off,' said Bimbo. 'We must look for our hooks or our buttons.'

'Where are they?' said Topsy, screwing herself round to have a good look down the middle of her back. 'I don't seem to remember them.'

'Well, they must be there somewhere,' said Bimbo. 'After all, we've got our fur coats *on*, haven't we? – so they must be buttoned round us somehow. I wonder who put them on us. I don't remember, do you?'

'No, I don't,' said Topsy, looking underneath herself to see if any buttons or hooks were there. 'It's really very funny where my buttons have gone, Bimbo. Have you found yours?'

'No,' said Bimbo, who was licking his fur to see if he could feel any buttons with his tongue. 'They must be hidden deep in our fur, Topsy. I'll hunt for yours, if you like. You'll tie yourself into a knot soon, trying to find them!'

So Bimbo hunted for the buttons that did up Topsy's fur coat – but no matter how he sniffed or licked, he couldn't find a single one! And when Topsy sniffed in Bimbo's coat, she couldn't find any either.

So they went to Bobs. 'Bobs, we want to take off our fur coats, because we're so hot,' said Bimbo.

'Well, take them off then,' said Bobs. 'I'm not stopping you. But go away and leave me alone, because I'm too hot even to talk.'

'Bobs, we can't find our coat buttons,' said Bimbo. 'Please will you look for them and undo them?'

'I can't find my own, so I'm certain I shan't find yours!' said Bobs, closing his eyes. 'Go away.'

The two animals went off sadly. Soon they met Cosy, and she laughed at their long faces. 'Whatever's the matter?' she said.

'We're so hot that we want to take off our coats,' said Topsy. 'But we don't know how to undo them.'

'Hold your breath hard, and maybe your buttons will go pop!' said Cosy. 'Then you can slip your coats off easily!' She laughed and ran off.

Then Bimbo and Topsy held their breaths and swelled themselves up, trying to make their buttons go pop. But they didn't. It was most disappointing.

Mistress came along just then, and was most astonished to see the kitten and the puppy behaving so strangely. 'What *do* you think you're doing?' she said.

'We're trying to take off our fur coats,' said Bimbo. 'We're so hot. Mistress, find our buttons and undo them, please. We want to be just in our skins, then we'll be cool.'

Mistress laughed. 'You silly little things!' she said. 'You can't take off your fur coats. They are growing on you!'

'But, Mistress, you take yours off!' said Topsy. 'Doesn't it grow on you, then?'

'Of course not, Bimbo!' said Mistress. 'We just have our skins and not fur like you. We put our clothes on top, and take them off when we like. It's a better idea than yours!'

'Well, Mistress, it may be a good idea in the summer,' said Topsy, 'but it's a *much* better idea to grow your own fur in the winter. You take my advice and do that. It's lovely and warm!'

But I don't expect Mistress will do anything of the sort, do you?

Chapter 12
Bobs Melts Away

The hot weather went on and on and on. The sun shone down more warmly every day, and the four animals tried their best to find the coolest places to lie in.

Bobs and Topsy hung their tongues out all day long. Bobs grew quite bad-tempered with the heat, and when Topsy and Bimbo wanted him to play with them, he snapped.

'Go away! Fancy talking about playing games when the sun is so hot. You must really be mad! Bones and biscuits, I'm melting away, as it is!'

'Are you really?' said Topsy, her soft brown eyes looking quite alarmed. 'Oh, Bobs, don't do that!'

'Well, I shall, if the sun gets much hotter,'

said Bobs. 'I shall just be a grease-spot on the ground. Then you'll be sorry you ever teased me or played tricks on me.'

Topsy and Bimbo ran off to find a cool place under a bush. 'Do you suppose Bobs really means what he says?' asked Topsy anxiously. 'Do you think he really *might* melt away?'

'Well, he's an old dog and a wise one, so I suppose he knows what he's talking about,' said Bimbo. 'He'd better keep out of the sun, I should think. It wouldn't be at all nice if he melted. I don't suppose he'd come back if he did.'

They lay in the cool for a little while, and then they heard Gillian calling them.

'Dinner, dinner, dinner! Dinner, dinner, dinner! Where are you all! Bobs, Cosy, Topsy, Bimbo! Dinner!'

Cosy jumped down from the wall and ran. Topsy and Bimbo rushed up to Gillian too. But there was no sign of Bobs.

'Do you think he heard?' said Topsy. 'He may be asleep.'

'Let's go and tell him,' said Bimbo. 'It's such a nice dinner. He won't like to miss it, and I'm afraid we shall eat it all if he doesn't come.'

So they ran to where they had last seen Bobs. But he wasn't there. 'He's gone some-where else,' said Topsy. And then she stopped and stared at something with very round eyes.

'What's the matter?' asked Bimbo.

'Look!' said Topsy, in alarm. 'Look on the ground there, near where Bobs was lying! There's something melting!'

Sure enough, near where Bobs had been,

a round spot of something melting in the
sun lay on the ground. The kitten and the
puppy stared at it in horror.

'He's done what he said – he's melted!'
said Topsy. 'Oh, poor, poor Bobs! He was so
hot that he melted!'

'We'd better tell Cosy,' said Bimbo, in a
trembling voice. 'Maybe she will be able to
do something about it.'

So they ran to Cosy, who was peacefully
picking out of one of the dishes the things
she liked most.

'Cosy! Come at once!' cried Bimbo.
'Something awful has happened to Bobs.
He's melted!'

'Don't be silly,' said Cosy. 'You only say
that because you want me to run off somewhere whilst you finish up the dinner. I know
you!'

'No, no, really it's true!' cried Bimbo.
'Bobs told us he felt like melting – and now
he has. There's nothing left of him but a
little round spot melting in the sun. Come
and see. It's dreadful.'

Cosy was alarmed. She ran with Topsy and
Bimbo and looked at the melting spot.

'Tails and whiskers!' she said. 'Tails and

whiskers! This is serious. Bobs is gone. Poor old Bobs! To think he should have melted away to nothing like that. We'd better be careful ourselves, and not lie about in the sun or we shall melt too.'

Topsy smelt at the spot on the ground. 'What's left of Bobs smells rather nice,' she said. The others smelt it too.

'Yes, it does smell good,' said Cosy, and she put out a tiny red tongue to have a lick.

'It tastes good too,' she said. 'Have a lick.'

And soon all three animals were licking up that melting spot as fast as they could. Then they sat down and looked sadly at one another.

'That's the end of Bobs,' said Topsy. 'We licked him up. I do feel unhappy.'

'So do I,' said Bimbo. 'We shall miss him.'

Just then there came the pitter-patter, pitter-patter of paws round the corner – and bones and biscuits, what a tremendous surprise – there was Bobs, staring in astonishment at the three animals.

'What in the world do you think you are doing?' he barked. 'Aren't you coming to have your dinner? Why are you sitting round in a ring, looking so miserable?'

'Well – we've just licked you up,' said Topsy, feeling muddled. 'You melted. See, that's where you melted.'

Bobs looked at the wet spot. 'You are a lot of sillies!' he wuffed. 'Really, you are. Gillian came along a little while ago carrying an ice-cream, and a piece of it fell just there. I went along with her because she said she'd give me a taste. I suppose you thought the bit of melting ice-cream was *me*! Well – I don't think it was very kind of you to lick me up, then! If I do melt away, I don't want to be licked up, thank you!'

And Bobs walked off in quite a huff. He wouldn't speak to the others for the rest of the day. Then Topsy promised that if ever Bobs did melt, she would never, never lick him up.

'All right,' said Bobs. 'I'll forgive you! Let's go and have a game!'

Chapter 13
A Very Peculiar Thing

Now one day Topsy felt very hungry indeed. She had been for a long walk by herself, and when she came back she ran to the place where the enamel bowls were.

There was no dinner in the first bowl she sniffed at. Bobs had eaten it all. There was nothing in the small bowl either, except a very delicious smell. Cosy and Bimbo had licked up everything there. She went to the third bowl where dry dog biscuits were always kept. There were nearly always some there – but that day there were none.

'Not a crumb!' wuffed Topsy to herself in dismay. 'This is too bad. I'm so terribly hungry – and there isn't even a lick round a plate for me.'

She sat down in a corner, lifted up her head and howled. It was a very sad and mournful howl. It made Bimbo jump. He was asleep in the next room, and at first he couldn't think what the noise was. Then it came again.

'Whoo-hoo-hoooooooooooh!   Whoo-hoo-oooooh!'

'My goodness – it's Topsy!' said Bimbo to himself in surprise. 'What is she making that noise for? Does she think she is singing a song?'

He ran out to see. Topsy was in the middle of another long 'Whoo-hooooooh!' her head well up in the air.

'Topsy! Are you singing?' cried Bimbo. 'I don't like your voice. Stop, do stop!'

'Whoo-hoo-hoooooooh!' wailed Topsy. 'I'm so hungry!'

'Well, find something to eat then,' said Bimbo crossly. 'Anyone would think you were Tommy Tucker singing for your supper, the noise you are making. You woke me up.'

'You're always sleeping,' said Topsy. 'I believe you would sleep all day and night if I didn't wake you up sometimes. Whoo-hoo-hoooooh!'

'Topsy, don't. That noise makes me shiver,' said Bimbo. 'Now let's see – what is there for you to eat?'

'Do you know anything anywhere that I can gobble up?' said Topsy, stopping her howling and looking at Bimbo. 'I'll share it with you if you can only tell me where to get something to eat. I'm so hungry I could almost eat your tail.'

'Now if you talk like that I won't think of anything,' said Bimbo, putting his tail under him and sitting down on it. 'Now – what do you feel like?'

'I feel like eating a long string of sausages,' said Topsy. 'Or three or four herrings. Or a joint of meat. Or a rabbit. Or a . . .'

'Well, you might know that all those things are impossible,' said Bimbo. 'I believe there's an old kipper head somewhere in the rubbish heap. What about that?'

'No good,' said Topsy gloomily. 'I ate that two days ago.'

'Well, what about that dirty old bone Bobs buried last week?' said Bimbo. 'You didn't want it then, but now that you're so hungry maybe you'd like it.'

'I would,' said Topsy, 'but I dug that up last Saturday and there's nothing left of it now.'

'If only we could find a cake or two in the nursery,' said Bimbo. 'Sometimes the children leave some on a plate. I could jump up on the table and see.'

'The nursery door is shut,' said Topsy. 'I've already been to see. But oh – doesn't a cake sound *nice*! A lovely crumby cake that I could gobble up. Oh, Bimbo – can't you possibly think where I can get a cake?'

Bimbo thought very hard indeed. Then his whiskers wagged a little, and his blue eyes sparkled.

'I know!' he said. 'I heard Gillian say this

morning that she had put a new cake of soap in the bathroom. I saw it too – it was round, like a cake, and it was pink. What about that, Topsy? It must be a cake of some sort, if Gillian called it a cake.'

'That sounds good,' said Topsy, cheering up. 'Let's go and get it.'

So off the two of them ran to the bathroom. There was no one there. Topsy put her front paws up on the basin to see where the cake of soap was. She saw it there, nice and round and pink. It really looked good enough to eat.

'I can't reach it,' she wuffed. 'Bimbo, you jump up and push it off for me.'

So up jumped Bimbo and down came the slab of slippery soap – plonk! It fell to the floor and Topsy picked it up in her mouth.

'It tastes a bit funny,' she said, and dropped it on the floor again. She sniffed at it. 'It smells sort of sweet, like the flowers in the garden,' she said, 'but it *does* taste a bit funny!'

'I expect it's the kind of cake that tastes lovely when it's bitten into,' said Bimbo. 'Give it a chew, Topsy, and see what it's like in the middle.'

So Topsy picked it up in her mouth again and gave it a good chew. But oh, she didn't at all like the taste. It was horrible.

'Bones and biscuits!' she wuffed. 'I can't eat it. I can't possibly eat it. It must be poisonous. Oh, I've got little bits left in my mouth. I must spit them out.'

But you know what soap does when it's wet – it froths up into a lather full of little bubbles, and that's just what happened to it inside Topsy's wet mouth!

Bimbo looked at Topsy in the greatest astonishment. 'Topsy! You are blowing bubbles!' he cried. 'Oh, you do look funny! Bubbles are coming out of your mouth. Look!'

Sure enough big and little bubbles flew out of Topsy's mouth as she breathed. The more she licked round her mouth to stop the bubbles, the more they came, for her mouth was full of soap.

'Fff-fff-fff-fff!' The bubbles kept on and on coming and Topsy was frightened. She ran out of the bathroom and went downstairs into the garden. There she met Bobs.

'Tails and whiskers!' cried Bobs. 'Whatever are you doing? Why are you blowing bubbles! Look – there they go flying away in the air! Have you got a bubble-pipe in your mouth, Topsy?'

'No, oh no!' wuffed poor Topsy, and as she barked, some great big bubbles flew out of her mouth. Some of them went POP on her whiskers and she didn't like that at all. 'I'm not blowing the bubbles – they are blowing themselves!'

Cosy ran up. 'Topsy is blowing bubbles!' she cried. Then up came Gillian and Imogen and they stared at the puppy in surprise.

'Mummy, come quick! Topsy is blowing bubbles out of her mouth!' shouted Imogen. 'She must have got some soap in her mouth.'

So Mistress came – and how she laughed when she saw poor Topsy puffing big and little bubbles out of her mouth every time she breathed.

'Poor little dog!' she said, 'You've been trying to eat soap. Don't you know that mustn't be eaten? Come with me and I'll put you right.'

Topsy put her tail down and went with Mistress. She had her mouth washed out with water till all the soap was gone. How

glad she was not to have to taste the horrible soap any more!

She ran to tell Bimbo. 'I'm all right again,' she wuffed. 'I'm not bubbling any more!'

'Topsy, Mistress has just put down some nice new dog biscuits in the bowl,' said Bimbo. 'Come and have them.'

But oh, wasn't it a pity – Topsy didn't feel hungry any more. 'I feel sick now,' she said, and her tail went down. 'I can't eat biscuits or anything. Bobs will eat them all.'

'Well, I'll hide a few under the rug in your basket,' said Bimbo, and he did. So, as soon as Topsy feels well enough to eat again, she will know where to go!

Chapter 14

When the Chimney Smoked

Once the nursery chimney wanted sweeping, and smoke began to pour out from the fire.

'What's happening!' cried Bobs. 'The fire keeps puffing smoke at me. I must go and tell the others.'

So off he ran as fast as he could, and met Topsy and Bimbo.

'The nursery fire is smoking!' he cried.

'What's it smoking?' asked Topsy in astonishment. 'A cigarette or a pipe?'

'Don't be silly,' said Bobs. 'It's just smoking. Come and see.'

So they all went to see, and the puppy and kitten were most astonished to see such enormous billows of smoke puffing out of the fireplace.

When Mistress saw all the smoke, she was quite upset. 'Look at that tiresome fire!' she said. 'The chimney is smoking. I must get the sweep.'

So she went for the sweep, and he came with his bundle of poles and his big round brush. The animals watched him in surprise.

'Isn't he black?' wuffed Topsy. 'Does he live in chimneys?'

'What's he going to do?' said Bimbo.

Gillian and Imogen came to watch the sweep. He put his brush on to the top of one of his poles, and pushed it up the chimney. Then he fitted on another pole and pushed the brush a bit higher. Then he fitted on a third pole.

'The poles send the brush higher and higher,' said Gillian, 'and it sweeps the chimney as it goes up. See the sweep twist his poles to send the brush round and round – that sweeps the chimney clean, Imogen.'

'If you go out into the garden, you will see my brush come suddenly out of the chimney,' said the sweep to the children. So they ran downstairs and into the garden. They looked up at the chimneys.

But no brush came. The animals all watched too. It was most disappointing. They didn't quite know which chimney was being swept, when they looked at them all on the roof, but they watched every one of them to see if the brush came popping out.

'Sweep! Your brush isn't coming out!' Imogen shouted up to the nursery window. The sweep popped his head out.

'It's got stuck,' he said. 'Maybe a brick has fallen out of the chimney. I'll have to push a bit.'

Bimbo was most interested in everything. 'I think I'll go up on the roof and have a closer view of what is happening,' he said. 'This is rather exciting. Coming, Topsy?'

'Don't be silly,' said Topsy. 'You know I can't climb. My jumping isn't much good, and my claws won't hold on to things as yours will. You go by yourself – but be careful.'

'Bimbo, you poke your nose into things too much,' said Bobs. 'You'd better not go up on the roof when a chimney is being swept. Why, even the chimney itself might fall on top of you.'

'I don't think so,' said Bimbo, and he went up on the roof at once. He first jumped on to the low garage roof, then on to the scullery roof, then ran up beside the kitchen chimney, then on to the big roof where all the other chimneys were.

'I'll look down them all and tell you which one the brush is in!' he called. 'That will be fun. Then you will know which one to watch.'

So the kitten jumped up first to the top of one big chimney and then to the top of another. He looked down them, but he

could see nothing. There was another big chimney just near by so he jumped up on that.

He looked down it – and at that very moment the sweep's brush shot up to the top of it and knocked poor Bimbo high into the air!

'Oh, look – the brush has come right out of that chimney!' shouted Gillian, 'and it has pushed Bimbo off – and, oh dear, he's gone into another chimney! He's fallen into it!'

Sure enough, poor Bimbo had disappeared into the chimney next to the nursery one. Plonk! He fell right into it and that was the last the children and the animals saw of him on the roof. They stood and waited for him to climb out, but he didn't.

'Oh well, I suppose he will come out when he is ready,' said Bobs. 'I expect he thinks we would all laugh at him if he climbed out now – and so we would. He'll come out when he thinks we're all safely indoors again!'

The sweep's brush disappeared down the chimney. A cloud of black soot hung over the roof for a minute or two and then disappeared.

'The fun's over,' said Bobs. 'We'll go indoors.'

So in they all went. Cosy curled up by the sitting-room fire and fell asleep. Bobs went to visit the cook in the kitchen to see if she was in a good temper. Topsy sat down and began to lick herself, for she felt a bit smoky from the nursery fire.

And, dear me, where was poor old Bimbo?

Chapter 15
The Very Strange Cat

Bimbo was in the chimney. He had fallen right into it, and had put out his claws to save himself as he tumbled down and down. He scrabbled against rough bricks, and at last landed on a ledge half-way down the chimney.

There was a pile of soot there, so it was soft to fall on. Bimbo sat there and tried to get back his breath. Soot flew all round him. It got into his eyes. It got on to his whiskers. It fell into his soft fur and made it as black as the next-door cat's coat.

Poor Bimbo! He coughed and spluttered, and felt very sorry for himself indeed. He sat on the ledge for a little while, trying to get used to the darkness around him. The chimney he was in led down to the cook's bedroom, and there was no fire in it at the moment, which was very lucky for Bimbo.

Bimbo looked up. Which was the best way to get out – to go up, or to go down? He really didn't know.

'Well, I came down from the top, so perhaps I'd better try to get back there,' thought the kitten at last. 'I know my way when I get out on to the roof – but goodness knows where this chimney leads to down there. It looks so dark and narrow.'

So he tried to climb upwards. But the chimney was very steep, and as fast as he climbed up, he fell back. Soot flew all around him and made him cough.

He sat on the ledge again and blinked his sooty eyes. He peered downwards. 'Well, I'll *have* to go down!' he thought. 'There's no other way. Here goes!'

And down he went, head-first, scrabble, scrabble, scratch, scratch, scratch! He fell right down to the fireplace in the cook's room.

The cook was there, doing her hair and putting on a clean apron. When she heard the noise in the chimney, she looked round at the fireplace in amazement.

Whatever could be happening?

Bimbo appeared. He was perfectly black from whiskers to tail. He opened his mouth and yowled pitifully, for he was very sorry for himself.

'What is it? It's a nasty little black imp!' cried the cook, and she tore out of her bedroom as fast as she could go. Bimbo ran after her, for he wanted to go down to the warm kitchen.

'It's after me, it's after me!' cried the cook, and she rushed downstairs at top speed. She ran into the kitchen and slammed the door. Bimbo was left outside, feeling very sad.

He wandered up the kitchen passageway and soon came to where Topsy was sitting down finishing the licking she was giving her paws. The puppy looked up and saw what looked like a black cat creeping slowly towards her.

Topsy jumped up at once and barked loudly. 'Wuff! What are *you* doing here! You don't belong here! Go away, strange cat, go away!'

The strange cat came closer. Topsy wuffed madly and sprang at it. The cat turned in fright and flew down the passageway to the garden, with Topsy after it. The cat jumped over the wall, and Topsy trotted back to the nursery, very pleased with herself.

'That will teach strange cats to come creeping into our house,' she thought, and curled herself up in her basket to have a sleep.

Poor Bimbo! He sat in the garden over the wall and felt very miserable. After a while he decided to go back to his own house. He

thought it was very, very unkind of Topsy to
have chased him like that.

He jumped back over the wall. He crept
quietly round the corner of the house and
went in at the garden door. Bobs and Cosy
were just trotting along together and they
saw him at once.

'Who's that?' cried Cosy. 'What a horrible-
looking cat! Chase him, Bobs, chase him!'

'Woooooooof!' barked Bobs in his loudest
voice, and tried to pounce on poor Bimbo.
Bimbo gave a loud yowl and fled away. Bobs
ran after him and Bimbo went up a tree.

'Woof, woof, woof!' barked Bobs at the
foot. 'Horrible, ugly, strange cat! Stay up
there in the tree! I'll bite you if you come
down!'

'Oh, don't be so unkind!' mewed Bimbo.
'I'm your friend, Bimbo. Stop barking and
listen to me.'

But every time that Bimbo tried to explain
who he was, Bobs barked all the more loudly,
and simply wouldn't listen. In the end
Bimbo curled himself up on a branch and
tried to make himself comfortable there. But
he couldn't.

So he stood up and shook himself – and a

shower of soot fell down, and made Bobs stare in surprise.

'What a peculiar cat!' he said to himself. 'He uses black powder! I'll go and tell Cosy to come and look.'

As soon as Bobs had trotted round the corner, Bimbo shot down the tree – but Bobs heard him land lightly on the ground and turned to chase him.

How Bimbo ran! He shot away like lightning, with Bobs at his heels, trying to snap at his long tail. Bimbo tried to jump up to the top of the greenhouse – but he just couldn't reach the glass roof, and he fell backwards.

SPLASH! He fell right into the rain-barrel at the side of the greenhouse. He disappeared into the water, and Bobs looked up in astonishment. He barked to Topsy and Cosy, who were running up.

'Cosy! Topsy! That horrid ugly black cat has fallen into the rain-barrel! Come and watch him climb out. We can catch him then.'

So the three of them sat around the rain-barrel and waited. Bimbo came up to the top of the water and splashed around a bit, trying to get out. He got to the side and climbed up. He shook himself.

Bobs and the others looked up at him. They looked and they looked!

'Now if this isn't a most extraordinary thing!' wuffed Bobs. 'A black cat falls into the water – and a different one comes out!'

'Magic!' said Cosy.

'It looks to me rather like old Bimbo,' said Topsy, sniffing.

'What! That drowned cat can't be Bimbo!' cried Bobs. 'No, no – Bimbo is somewhere down that chimney still.'

'Mee-ow-ee-yow, ee-yow!' wailed poor Bimbo. 'I *am* Bimbo! I am, I am! I'm not a strange, ugly, black cat – I'm your own Bimbo, very miserable and wet and unhappy.'

'Bones and biscuits! I really do believe it *is* Bimbo!' cried Cosy. 'Bimbo! Where have you been?'

'Down the chimney,' wailed Bimbo. 'And nobody believed it was me when I came out. The cook called me a black imp and ran away when I landed in her bedroom – and you all chased me and called me names. But I'm Bimbo just the same.'

'He must have been black with soot,' said

Bobs, 'and that's why we didn't know him. What a good thing you fell into the water, Bimbo, and got the black soot washed off you, or we might never have known you again! Come along down. We won't chase you any more.'

So poor, shivering Bimbo jumped down – and what a fuss was made of him for the rest of that day. He had all the titbits out of the dinner-dish, and the warmest place by the fire. He *did* enjoy himself!

Chapter 16
The Moon in the Pail

One night the moon was full. It hung in the sky like a great, white globe, and shone marvellously. The four animals were astonished at it.

'I wonder who hung that lamp in the sky

tonight,' said Bobs. 'It's lighting up the whole garden. It's wonderful. I like it.'

'Do you see how it sails in and out of the clouds?' said Cosy. 'I'd like to do that. It would be fun.'

'I wish I had the moon for my own,' said Topsy. 'I would like such a lovely thing to play with. I would roll it down the garden path, and it would give me a light wherever it went. Oh, I do wish I had it.'

'I'll get it for you,' grinned Bimbo. 'What will you give me if I do?'

'I'll give you the big bone that the butcher boy threw to me this morning,' said Topsy, after she had thought for a while. 'That's what I'll give you. I've hidden it away and nobody knows where it is. But I'll give it to you if you really will get me the moon to play with.'

'Right!' said Bimbo, and ran off. He came to where the cook had stood an empty pail outside the kitchen door. He dragged it to the garden tap and filled the pail full of water.

The reflection of the bright moon shone in the pail of water. It looked lovely there, round and bright, just like the moon in the sky.

Bimbo waited until the water was quite still, and the moon shone there, round and beautiful. Then he ran off to find Topsy.

'Topsy!' he mewed. 'I've got the moon for you. Come and see.'

'Oh, where!' cried Topsy in delight, and ran off with Bimbo to the pail.

'Look in my pail of water,' said Bimbo. 'Do you see the moon there? Well, you can have it.'

'Yes – it's really there,' said Topsy, looking at the reflection of the bright moon there. It really did look exactly as if the moon had fallen into the pail! 'Oh, Bimbo, how good and clever you are to get me the moon, as I asked. But why did you put it into a pail of water?'

'Well, it might have got out if it hadn't got water over it,' said Bimbo at once. 'Now, Topsy, remember your promise – where's that big bone you hid away?'

'I'll show you,' said Topsy, and she took Bimbo to where the yew hedge grew. She dug about a little and sniffed. Then she began to scrabble and scrape for all she was worth, and at last, up came the great big juicy bone that the butcher boy had given to

Topsy for herself. It was rather dirty, but Bimbo didn't mind that! He took it in his mouth and ran off.

'You go and play with your moon!' said Bimbo, with a laugh. So off Topsy went to the pail of water. The moon still swam there, round and bright. Topsy sat down and looked into the water. 'Come on out, Moon,' she said. 'I want to play with you. Come out, and I will roll you down the path like a big shining ball, and every little mouse and hedgehog, every beetle and worm, will come out to watch you rolling by!'

But the moon didn't come out. It stayed in the pail and shone there, silvery bright.

'Do come out!' begged Topsy. 'Please do. It must be so horrid and cold there in the water – and so wet, too. That's the horrid thing about water – it's always so wet. If it was dry, it would be much nicer to bathe in.'

The moon shone there, but it didn't come out. Topsy grew angry.

'Do you want me to put my nose into the water and get you out?' she barked. 'You won't like that. I might nip you with my teeth, Moon. Come along out, do!'

But the moon didn't. Topsy sat and looked

at it, with her head on one side. 'Well, I shall put in my nose then,' she said. 'And I shall get hold of you. So look out!'

She put her nose into the water and tried to get hold of the moon. But, of course, the moon wasn't really there, so all that poor Topsy got was a mouthful of water that made her choke and cough. She was very angry.

'Do you know what I am going to do?' she wuffed. 'I am going to tip the pail over – then the water will run out and away, and you will find yourself on the ground for me to play with!'

So Topsy tipped over the pail, and out went the water with a gurgling noise all over the ground. Topsy waited to jump on the moon – but what a peculiar thing, no moon came out of the pail!

'Where's it gone, where's it gone?' howled Topsy, scraping about the ground as if she thought the moon was stuck there. 'She was in the water – and the water's out, but the moon isn't.'

'Whatever is the matter?' said Bobs, wandering up. 'What are you doing dancing round that empty pail, Topsy? Have you suddenly gone mad?'

'No,' said Topsy. 'But a very sad thing has happened, Bobs. Bimbo got the moon and put her into a pail of water for me. I tipped up the pail to get the moon out – but somehow she's slipped away and gone. I can't find her.'

'Well, I know where she's gone,' said Bobs, with a sudden giggle.

'Where?' said Topsy, in surprise.

'Back to the sky. Look!' said Bobs. And when Topsy looked up into the sky, sure enough there was the bright round moon sailing along between the clouds as quickly as ever!

'Well! To think she jumped back there so quickly!' said Topsy, in surprise. 'Bimbo! Bimbo! Give me back my bone! The moon's got out of the pail and has gone back to the sky!'

But Bimbo was nowhere to be found. Neither was the bone! I'm not at all surprised, are you?

Chapter 17
A Surprise for Bimbo

Once Bimbo went creeping into the kitchen to see if there were anything he could eat. Sometimes the cook dropped things on the floor, and if she couldn't stop to pick them up at that moment, there was just a chance that any animal under the table could snap them up!

'Cook dropped a bit of bacon rind yesterday,' thought Bimbo. 'And once she dropped a sausage! Maybe she will drop a haddock today, or something really exciting!'

So he sat patiently under the table and waited and waited. But all that the cook dropped was a fork that stuck into Bimbo's tail, and he didn't like that at all!

He was just going away when the cook

went into the scullery to answer the back door. Bimbo jumped up on to the table at once. Cook was making cakes – but there was nothing there for Bimbo to eat. He didn't want flour. He didn't want sugar. He didn't want currants.

But wait a minute – what was this? There was a little jug of milk on the table – and oh, the cream on the top of that milk!

'Now this is something worth having!' thought Bimbo in delight, and he put his head down to the jug. He put out his pink tongue – but alas, it couldn't reach the cream, because the jug was only half full.

'Well, there's nothing for it but to put my head into the jug and lick the milk like that,' thought Bimbo. He took a quick look into the scullery. Good – the cook was still talking to the butcher-boy. So into the neck of the jug went Bimbo's little head, and he began to lick up the cream greedily.

Then he heard the cook bang the scullery door and he knew she was coming back. What a scolding he would get if she found him stealing the milk. He tried to take his head out of the jug at once – but he couldn't! It was stuck!

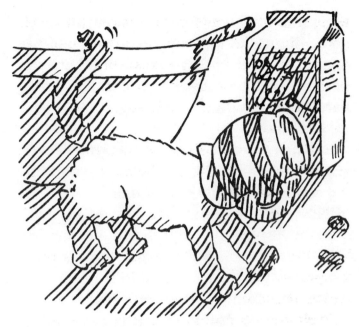

He tried and tried. He heard the cook coming back into the kitchen. Poor Bimbo! He jumped down from the table with his head still in the jug. Milk poured all over him!

He ran quickly out of the door, banging himself on the side of it as he went, because, of course, he couldn't see with his head inside the jug!

Down the passageway he ran, and came to the little room where Mistress often worked. He thought he would go in there and work the jug off his head in peace. He slipped inside the room and sat down, panting, the jug still over his head. It was hard to breathe properly with it on, and it felt very tight and uncomfortable.

'The milk has soaked my face,' thought Bimbo. 'It is perfectly horrid. I don't like it at all. I am very unhappy. Now – before anyone comes, I really *must* try to drag this jug off my head. My front paws will help me.'

So Bimbo sat and tried to pull the jug off his head with his paws. But it simply wouldn't come!

'Bones and biscuits, tails and whiskers, whatever in the world am I to do?' thought poor Bimbo, in a fright. 'Have I got to wear this jug all the rest of my life? I do hope not. I'd better go and find Topsy and see if she will pull it off for me.'

So off he went out of the little room to find Topsy. He couldn't see at all where he was going, and he kept bumping into the wall making a tremendous noise.

Bang-bang, bang-crash, he went. Topsy heard the strange noise and pricked up her ears. She ran to see what it was. Bimbo heard the pitter-patter of her paws and called out to Topsy. 'Topsy, help me! Topsy, help me!'

But the jug made his voice sound very odd indeed – just like yours sounds when you roll up a paper and then talk down it. 'Wop-wop-wop-wop!' his voice sounded like. 'Wop-wop-wop-wop!'

Topsy stared and listened in the greatest astonishment. What could this creature be with a jug for a head and a voice that said 'Wop-wop-wop-wop!' all the time? Topsy didn't like it. She put her tail down and fled away to find Bobs and Cosy.

Bimbo clattered after her, the jug bumping against the walls as he ran. Topsy found Bobs and cosy and wuffed to them.

'There's a jug-headed animal in the house that says 'Wop-wop-wop-wop!' in a funny deep voice. I'm frightened! Save me!'

'Don't be silly,' said Bobs, getting up. 'A jug-headed animal with a voice that says 'Wop-wop!' You must be mad!'

But when Bimbo came round the corner with the jug still on his head, crying for help in a voice that still sounded exactly like 'Wop-wop-wop!' – all the three animals were as scared as could be. They fled into the garden at once. And out into the garden after

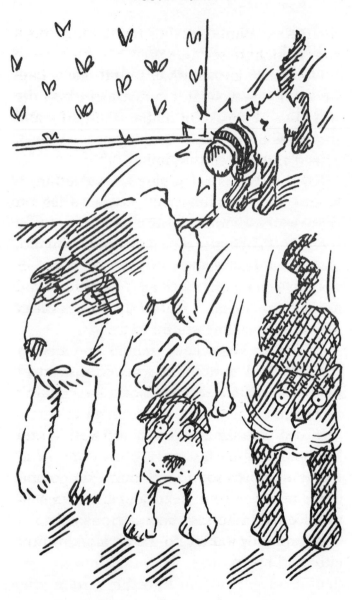

them went Bimbo, crying for help. It was a strange sight to see.

Goodness knows what would have happened if Bimbo hadn't run straight into the wall. The jug broke in half and fell off – and there was Bimbo's face looking at the others, scared and soaked with milk.

'Bimbo! Is this a new game or something?' cried Bobs. 'Whatever did you put a jug on your head for? You gave us an awful fright.'

'I didn't put it on,' said poor Bimbo, beginning to wash his face clean. 'It wouldn't come off, that's all. And I think you are a lot of mean creatures, running away when I kept calling out for help.'

'Well, we *would* have helped you if only you had said something sensible instead of 'Wop-wop-wop-wop!' said Topsy. 'We couldn't think what that meant, so we ran away.'

'I did *not* say 'Wop-wop-wop-wop!'' said Bimbo. 'But maybe the jug over my head made my words sound like that. You go and get a jug over your head and talk down it, and see what it sounds like, one of you.'

But nobody wanted to – and don't you try either, will you!

Chapter 18
Christmas at Last!

'Christmas is coming,' said Bobs to Bimbo and Topsy.

'Who's he?' asked Topsy. 'A visitor?'

'No, silly,' said Bobs. 'Christmas is a day – we all get presents and everyone is happy.'

'Who brings the presents?' asked Bimbo.

'Santa Claus, of course,' said Bobs.

'Any relation of mine?' asked Bimbo, stretching out his twenty claws for everyone to see. 'I'm Bimbo Claws, as you can see. Is Santa Claus an uncle of mine, do you think?'

'Don't be funny,' said Bobs. 'Santa Claus is a kind old gentleman. Gillian and Imogen call up the chimney to tell him what they want in their Christmas stockings. They hang up a stocking each, and Santa Claus fills it on

Christmas Eve. We had better hang up stockings too – it would be lovely to find bones and chocolate and biscuits in them, wouldn't it!'

'That seems a very good idea,' said Bimbo, sitting up. 'Did you say this nice old gentleman lives up the chimney?'

'No, I didn't,' said Bobs. 'I said that the children call up the chimney to tell him what they want.'

'Well, if he can hear them, he must be up the chimney then,' said Topsy. 'Bimbo, you're used to chimneys. You climb up them all, one by one, and see which one Santa Claus lives in.'

'No, thank you,' said Bimbo. 'No more chimneys for me. We'll call up, though, and say what we want, shall we?'

'And we'll hang up stockings too,' said Cosy.

'We haven't got any,' said Topsy. 'We don't wear them. Can't we hang up our collars instead?'

'I suppose you think our collars would easily hold things like biscuits and chocolates?' said Bobs. 'I do think you are silly sometimes, Topsy.'

'Well, you be clever and tell us what to do about stockings then,' said Topsy, snapping at Bobs' tail.

'Don't do that,' said Bobs. 'Let me think a minute. Oh – I know!'

'What?' cried Topsy, Bimbo and Cosy.

'Well, you know that the children's stockings are hung up on the line to dry, don't you?' said Bobs. 'Well, what about jumping up and getting some for ourselves? We can easily do that!'

So the next day all four of them went to look at the clothes line. And, sure enough, there were two pairs of long stockings there – one belonging to Imogen and one to Gillian. It wasn't long before Bobs was jumping up to get hold of one.

But he couldn't get high enough. So Topsy tried. She caught hold of a stocking with her teeth. She hung on for all she was worth – and, oh dear, the clothes line broke, and all the clothes fell in a heap on poor Topsy!

How scared she was! She tore off down the garden, with the line wound round her body – and all the clothes galloped after her!

It was the funniest sight to see. Bobs, Cosy

and Bimbo sat down and laughed till they cried. But when Mistress came out and saw how all the clean clothes were dragged in the mud, she wasn't a bit pleased. Topsy got a scolding and sat and sulked all by herself in the corner. 'That was a very bad idea of yours,' she said to Bobs.

But when Christmas Eve came, what a lovely surprise! Gillian and Imogen came into the nursery with four stockings and showed them to the surprised animals.

'You shall hang up your stockings just as we do!' said Imogen. 'Here is one for you, Bobs – and one for you, Topsy – and smaller ones for the cats.'

The four stockings were hung just above the animals' baskets. They did look funny, hanging limp and thin and empty.

'If you go to sleep, and don't peep, perhaps Santa Claus will come down the chimney here in the night and fill these stockings for you,' said Imogen. 'Perhaps you will have a new collar, Bobs – and you a rubber bone, Topsy – and you a ball to roll about, Bimbo – and you a new rug for your basket, Cosy. And maybe you will have biscuits and sardines and bones and other nice things as well! So

go to sleep and don't make a sound, in case
you frighten Santa Claus away!'

'Isn't this exciting?' said Topsy, when the
children had gone out of the room. 'I'm
going to settle down in my basket and go to
sleep straight away!'

'So am I,' said Bimbo. 'Oooh – I do hope I
shall get a tin of sardines. I wonder if Santa
Claus will have any in his sack?'

'I really *would* love a new collar,' said Bobs.
'Mine is so old. Well – goodnight to you all.

I'm going to sleep too. And if we hear old Father Christmas, we mustn't peep! Do you hear, Topsy? No peeping!'

'Well, don't you peep either,' said Topsy. 'And don't think he is a robber or something when he comes, and bark at him, or you'll frighten him away! Goodnight, everyone!'

And very soon all the animals were fast asleep. Bobs and Cosy were curled up together in one big basket, and Bimbo and Topsy were fast asleep in the small one.

They dreamt that their stockings were full of all the things that animals love – bones and biscuits, sardines and kippers, balls and saucers of cream. Ooooooh!

Chapter 19
A Happy Christmas!

In the morning the four animals awoke. Topsy woke first and put her head out of the basket. She sniffed hard. She could smell a lovely smell.

'Oh! It's Christmas morning!' she wuffed in Bimbo's ear. Bimbo woke up with a jump.

'What about our stockings?' he said. 'Did Santa Claus come in the night? I didn't hear him.'

'LOOK!' cried Bobs, waking up too. 'Our stockings are crammed full! I can smell bones.'

'And I can smell sardines!' cried Cosy. All the animals got out of their baskets and sniffed round the exciting stockings.

'A new collar for me!' barked Bobs, drag-

149

ging one out in delight. 'Just look at it –
brass studs all the way round. My word, I
shall look grand. I wish I had a tie to go with
it, like men wear.'

'A rubber bone for me!' wuffed Topsy, and
she took the bone from her stocking and
tried to chew it. But the more she chewed at
the bone, the less she seemed to eat of it.
Most peculiar!

'That bone will last you for years,' said
Bobs with a grin. 'It's all chew and no taste!
Give me a real bone any day!'

'A fine new ball for me!' mewed Bimbo,
rolling a lovely red ball over the floor. 'Come
and play with me, Topsy. Throw it into the
air and make it bounce.'

'What about my new rug?' said Cosy, drag-
ging a knitted rug into her basket and lying
down on it. 'Now this is what I call a really
fine present. I shall be able to lie on it and
keep myself warm, and you, Bobs, will be
able to hide all kinds of goodies under it, to
keep till you want them.'

'What, hide them under your rug for you
to nibble at when I'm not there!' cried Bobs.
'No, thank you, Cosy. Oh, tails and whiskers,
there are other things in our stockings too –

look! A real big bone for me, full of crunch and nibble!'

'And there's a tin of sardines for me and Bimbo,' said Cosy. 'Oh, I hope Gillian and Imogen come along quickly to open it. I just feel as if I could do with three or four sardines inside me.'

'There are biscuits at the bottom of *my* stocking,' said Topsy, putting her head right down to the bottom of the stocking and nosing about in the toe. 'Biscuits! Big ones and little ones! I'll give you each one if you like.'

She got some into her mouth – but, dear me, when she wanted to take out her head and give the biscuits to the others, she couldn't get rid of the stocking. It stuck fast over her head and Topsy ran about the room in the stocking. The others did laugh!

Then in came Gillian and Imogen. 'Happy Christmas, Bobs, Topsy, Bimbo and Cosy!' they cried. 'Oh, Topsy, whatever are you doing? What are you wearing that stocking on your head for? Did you think it was a hat?'

They pulled the stocking from Topsy's head, and the four animals crowded round the children to thank them for their lovely presents. Topsy was glad to have her head out of the stocking. 'I felt like you did when you wore the jug,' she said to Bimbo.

'Here's a bar of chocolate for you two girls,' said Bobs, and he pulled one out from his basket. 'I've sat on it for the last week, I'm afraid, so it's a bit squashy, but the taste is still there, because I've tried it each morning.'

'And here's one of my very Best Biscuits,' said Topsy, fetching one from her basket. 'It's the biggest one I have had in my dinner bowl for weeks. Try it. I've nibbled a pattern all round the edge to make it pretty for you.'

'And I've been into the hen-run and collected you a few feathers,' said Cosy. 'I hope they'll be useful. Good gracious, Bimbo – whatever *have* you got there?'

'My collection of kipper-heads from the rubbish-heaps all round,' said Bimbo proudly. 'They're the best I could find. I hid them in the landing cupboard in a hat box there.'

'Gracious! That was what made that awful smell, I suppose!' said Gillian. 'And, oh dear, Bimbo – Mummy keeps one of her best hats in that box. I can't imagine what she'll say if she goes out smelling of kippers.'

'I should think she'll be very pleased,' said Bimbo. 'Kippers have a gorgeous smell. I'm surprised people don't make scent of them, instead of silly things like honeysuckle and sweet-peas!'

'Well, thank you all very much,' said Gillian. 'You've given us lovely presents. Now let's all go to breakfast, and we'll show you the presents *we* had too!'

So off they all went, Bobs wearing his new collar, and Topsy carrying her rubber bone for another long chew. Cosy had to leave her rug behind, but Bimbo rolled his ball all the way to the dining-room.

The sardines were opened, and Cosy and Bimbo shared them with the dogs.

'Delicious,' they all said, and licked their whiskers clean.

They had a lovely Christmas, and even had a taste of the great big turkey. They had a special supper that evening of biscuits soaked in turkey gravy, and then, full of good things, they all went to their baskets to sleep.

They curled up together, put their noses between their paws, and dreamed lovely dreams of sardines, bones, collars and balls!

And there we will leave them, dreaming happily, a contented little family of four. Happy days to all of them, and especially to dear old Bimbo and Topsy!

A letter from Topsy

Hello, children!

Well, you've read our book from beginning to end now – and I do hope you liked it. Aren't we a mischievous lot of animals? But all the same I am sure you would like to have a game with us if you lived near by.

Come and live next door, won't you? That would be fine. Then we'd all come and see you, and you could tell us what to put into our next book. We'd teach you to play chase-your-tail and bark-at-the-moon and snap-at-legs. You'd love that!

Barks and licks from,

Topsy

Happy Days — Enid Blyton

978-0-75372-578-8

978-0-75372-579-5

978-0-75372-581-8

978-0-75372-580-1

978-0-75372-582-5

978-0-75372-584-9

978-0-75372-583-2

978-0-75372-585-6

978-0-75372-586-3

Enid Blyton

You're a Nuisance Mister Meddle

Happy Days

978-0-75372-577-1

Enid Blyton

The Adventures of Mr Pink-Whistle

Happy Days

978-0-75372-587-0

Enid Blyton

Mr Pink-Whistle Has Some Fun

Happy Days

978-0-75372-588-7

Enid Blyton

Mr Pink-Whistle's Party

Happy Days

978-0-75372-589-4

Enid Blyton

Mr Pink-Whistle Interferes

Happy Days

978-0-75372-590-0

Enid Blyton

Hello Mr Twiddle!

Happy Days

978-0-75372-591-7

Enid Blyton

Mr Twiddle in Trouble Again

Happy Days

978-0-75372-592-4

Enid Blyton

Don't Be Silly, Mr Twiddle

Happy Days

978-0-75372-593-1

Enid Blyton

Well, Really, Mr Twiddle!

Happy Days

978-0-75372-594-8